MW01119903

CALLED TO THE KINGDOM

Amelia Susan

**To Contact
Amelia Susan
Email:
thehealingplace@cabletv.on.ca**

PRESS

Dedication

This compilation of writings began simply as expressions and movements within my heart and spirit that spilled out onto paper. It is only through the patient and gentle leading of the Holy Spirit that these writings have been penned, gathered together, and published. So it is to The Most High that I present this book and ask that His presence, power, and Kingdom be made manifest to those whom these pages reach. As well, I would like to thank my husband, Norman — my gift from God — for his encouragement, patience, and support throughout this entire process which the Father has taken us.

— Amelia Susan

Contents

Strength for the Journey

Introduction

Called to the Kingdom may not be for you if you are already comfortable in your Christian walk and do not want to take the risks involved with going deeper into the Kingdom with Jesus Christ.

Inside these covers are insights into the spiritual realm, where those who are true warriors in the Kingdom of God see beyond this world and battle forces of darkness.

This book will expose you to the reality of life as a battle-scarred warrior living beyond the safety net of organized religion while fulfilling their destiny in Christ.

You may be shocked, offended, and have your insulated world as a 'practicing Christian' shattered.

Read at your own risk! The risk of giving up the life you now have to live dangerously as a warrior for Jesus Christ.

LIFE IN THE KINGDOM

Welcome to the Kingdom

The day was bright and sunny—a beautiful, hot, mid-summer day—a perfect day to pack the family into the van and travel to the nearest water park. On arrival, we eagerly donned our bathing suits, grabbed our towels and water bottles, and headed for the water slides.

The place was crowded—not to our surprise on such a perfectly hot day. Many rides caught our attention and we enjoyed them all—screaming, laughing, and getting completely soaked. There was one ride which, near the end of a day of trying all the other rides, looked quite appealing—especially to the tired, the weary, or the slightly more 'age-advantaged' visitors to the park. No matter, it seemed to be the final ride of choice for all at the end of a wonderful day. Fittingly, it was named "The Lazy River". With only one entrance, the people filed down the ramp one by one, each receiving a brightly coloured inner tube to crawl onto as they began their journey.

Some splashed and kicked. Others just relaxed and enjoyed the effortless ride around the bends and curves, gently weaving through the park. Some enjoyed the occasional excitement of a waterfall that woke them from their restful ride for a few brief moments—and then the current would continue to carry them along the canal that had carried so many visitors before them. Sometimes people would get off their tube and walk in the river a bit. Others might change tubes with someone else or jump onto another's tube just for something to do—to add some excitement to what may have been for the more energetic a bit of a boring ride—at least compared to the wilder rides enjoyed earlier.

Nonetheless, nothing seemed to be able to completely thwart the current of the lazy river, gently pushing and jostling the people-laden rafts toward the end of the ride which seemed to come so quickly. The exit was at the same place as the entrance. Those in line-ups were continuing to slowly descend the ramp step by step and take their place on the tube and proceed to go around the river again and again and again. Entering—riding—exiting—entering—riding—exiting—altering the experience only slightly through pushing against other tubes or floating under waterfalls, but all inevitably traveling the same path and ultimately disembarking at the same place, only to ride the river again.

No one dared to swim across the channel and crawl up onto the grassy rest area surrounded by the lazy river to bathe in the warm sun. They probably would have been asked to come back and leave the ride. 'The administration' wouldn't want everybody doing that—it would upset the flow of the tubes. It would distract the other riders. It might cause some chaos and confusion for those on their safe and predictable journey around the river.

Sometimes, it seems that our pursuit of the kingdom of God is likened to a ride on the lazy river. Many believers ride many different tubes over and over again—trying, hoping, striving—to experience the kingdom of God. Their intentions are good. They sincerely desire to abide and rest in the kingdom—to experience the joy and peace of the kingdom. Perhaps if they climb into the tube of ministry, the kingdom will not be far down the river. After all, there are myriads of ministries out there—children's, teen's, young adult's, single's, divorced, married couple's, retired laymen, retired minister's, and on and on the list of potential ministries goes. Perhaps if they serve for many years on a board of deacons, the kingdom of God will open for them. Some exchange their 'tubes' for a different one, thinking that a change may be just what they are looking for. Perhaps years spent in the nursery or on the hospitality committee will do it. Or how about filling the office of a Sunday school superintendent or even the treasurer?

Frantically and nearing exhaustion, some well-intentioned believers hop from one tube to the next, hoping this one will be 'it'—the one that takes them closer to the King. The one service that opens the gates of heaven so they can experience what 'everyone else' seems to experience—that amazing vision, that supernatural encounter, or maybe that extra-ordinary, divine intervention. "I need it so bad!" they tell themselves. They feel they are the only ones who have never encountered God outside of simple prayer and Bible reading. They've strived and served and sacrificed for years and years but still the current of the river continues to bump them along the channel, through the same bends and curves and occasional waterfall, all coming to the end of the ride—ironically where another trip around the river begins again.

"How do I get across to the kingdom?" they ask themselves. "I know there must be something more. I know. I can sense the presence of the Most High there. I can see the brightness of His glory shining over the land there. What am I doing wrong? I'm doing what so many others have done for so many years before me. Have they been to the Kingdom yet? Inside I know. I am driven. I'm drawn to the center. I must get to the Kingdom. I know there is more."

In shear desperation and almost total exhaustion, this desperate soul, hungering for more—more of the Kingdom of God—jumps into the river without a tube. Guards warn them to turn around and get a tube like the rest or exit the river. Whistles are blown. Everyone stops and all eyes are fixed on the one who is not following the 'rules of the river'.

Desperately, with arms flailing and fighting against the current while pushing the tubes out of the way, they make it to the other side. They drag themselves up onto the embankment. With chest throbbing—lungs grasping for air—they crawl up the grassy bank. Farther and farther from the clamor of the river, sounds of whistles and pleas for their return to the safety of the rafts in the river drift into the background.

Head hidden in their arms, they rest for a moment. They feel something—a deep penetrating warmth begins to wash over their body. Their breathing regulates and they begin to gain strength—enough to raise their head and look about. Looking up, their eyes gaze into His beautiful face. Peace and rest flood into their soul.

"Am I in the Kingdom? Did I find the Kingdom of God or have I died?" their thoughts race.

"Yes," comes the reply. "You are in the Kingdom and 'Yes,' you have died—died to striving, died to struggle, died to performance, expectation, and accomplishment, died to self. Now you can 'live'— with Me—in the Kingdom. Live in peace surpassing all circumstances, live in joy in the midst of struggle and testing, live in righteousness, having your mind, soul, and spirit continually washed and renewed with My blood."

"You are alive—free to enjoy this world, free to follow Me and listen to My voice above all others, free to move and live and have your being found in Me. You have come alive to the awareness that all I desire is you—-neither your service nor your accomplishments—just **you** to love Me with all your heart and soul and mind."

"Watch as I flow through your heart, changing your motivation for service to that of a desire for others to see and abide in the Kingdom. Watch as I flow through your spirit, awakening it to another realm—not of flesh and blood—but a spiritual realm where you are trained to be a warrior—a super-conqueror—setting yourself and others free to live in freedom, victory, peace, and joy of the Holy One."

"Welcome to the Kingdom."

Kingdom Walk

There is, these days, so much talk of the kingdom. Many desire to walk in the kingdom, to develop a 'kingdom mentality,' to live and breathe in this 'other place'.

We have heard the kingdom of God is here—the kingdom of God is within us. What is it to walk in the kingdom of God? Does it mean to live with disregard to the responsibilities of your life—work, children, school, bills, spouses, and relationships? I do not believe Jesus calls us to His kingdom to live in a fantasy land while neglecting the gifts of family and relationships or to ignore the responsibility of providing for and instructing those with whom we have in or under our charge. Jesus does not call us to some 'altered state' of existence where we walk around like spiritual zombies unable to function in our modern world because our heads are in the clouds. We are to be salt and light to this place in which we live.

When we fill ourselves with the presence of God—when we submerge our body, soul, and spirit into His enveloping energy—then He begins to transform us from the inside. We slowly begin to develop spiritual senses.

One of these senses is Kingdom ears—listening to the voice of our Shepherd—to hear and believe His voice when He tells us of His love for us, when He speaks to our hearts to encourage and strengthen our faith, to hear His heart speak to us and inspire us to follow hard after Him with all our being, calling us to surrender ourselves to Him—to cast our cares on Him.

Kingdom ears also discern the voice of darkness that speaks chaos, confusion, and destruction—those dark sinister words that cut deep into our soul and spirit bringing condemnation and thoughts of worthlessness—voices from the prince of the power of the air that carry words of hate and death and woo us to abandon the sweet pure call of the Saviour and try to turn our mind and heart away from the voice of Truth and Life.

When Jesus has tuned your ears to His voice and you can discern His leading, then you will notice that things are not as they once appeared. In fact, not all things are as they appear at all. Kingdom eyes begin to focus, seeing through the Master's eyes, recognizing darkness as it moves through those in your home, in your office, in your school, and in your church—recognizing unclean spirits parasiting off of unsuspecting hosts, hoping to remain unnoticed as they hop from one to another to do more damage. Keep alert! The devil roams around like a roaring lion seeking those he can devour. Kingdom eyes allow you to navigate through your daily life while being watchful and ready to do combat with the enemy, making no allowance for him to gain entry into your body, soul (heart, will, and emotions) or spirit.

There is a sweet blessing from kingdom eyes, especially if they're governed by a kingdom heart— a heart whose total being is captivated by the love of the Father—who is so embraced in His strong secure arms that their heart is free and safe and able to let go of striving to obtain His attention. This is truly a soul who has found peace. Not a striving, anxious heart always looking about to see who's doing what and where, and then comparing it to themselves. Not a fretful heart that questions, "Is God using them more? Does He show them more of Himself or manifest more of His glory through them? Does He love them more because they're doing such and such and I'm not?"

This heart must stop beating—must actually die—cease to function—because a kingdom heart is a transplant heart—a new heart—specially carved and formed and infused with the blood of life and love from the Lord Jesus Christ Himself, where every beat is dedicated to loving Jesus, where every desire is to praise and glorify the King, and where every longing is to see the kingdom of God unfold like the petals of a beautiful rose in a dark and dying world.

Hearts that have been saturated with Jesus are able to recognize the hand of the Saviour working in and through the lives of others and are able to rejoice with them. Kingdom hearts also encourage others to exercise their gifts; to 'show and tell' what God is accomplishing through them. At times it seems some believers are starved for attention and acceptance and to gain such, they each clamor to the teacher, pushing others out of the way to get to be the one up front to show their 'find'—their treasure. Kingdom hearts don't push and shove but esteem others more highly than themselves. They take the little ones by the hand and lead them up to the front of the class and let them share with joy and excitement the treasure they have found in Jesus. Kingdom hearts say, "What a fine treasure! You make the Son shine. Go, now, and search for more treasure, and come back to tell us and show us what you have found."

There's plenty of room at the Father's knee for all His children to bring their treasures to share. Have a heart—a kingdom heart—and encourage the little ones to come unto the Father for of such is the kingdom of God. (Matthew 19:14)

To walk in the kingdom is to walk this earth as an alien for your eyes, ears, and heart are operating in two realms. There is a spiritual awareness that more is going on than what appears. You are continually watching yet spiritually perceiving the moving of the Holy Spirit; listening yet carefully discerning the Master's voice. You desire to strengthen and encourage other kingdom dwellers, and you are always vigilant — always on the lookout — for those who need to meet Jesus — the King.

The King knows the desire of our hearts, and He will faithfully guide us as we travel more and more into the kingdom — our hand securely in His. "I will set the Lord continually before me; because He is at my right hand, I will not be shaken." (Psalm 16:8)

Extreme Living

If you are acquainted with the history of the far North, you will no doubt be familiar with one of the most exciting and daring times—that being the Gold Rush Era.

Optimistic entrepreneurs would sell all they had to purchase their supplies and travel countless miles over rugged, unfamiliar terrain in unpredictable weather just to hammer their stake into a piece of property they bought sight unseen, solely on speculation.

With great hope and anticipation, they set up camp and began the arduous task of digging and panning for gold. Often they would spend countless weeks and months and, for some, maybe years digging and panning and sifting through mud and river beds or tunneling into hills, hoping they would soon hold their sought-after treasure in their hands.

Lonely, hungry, and at the mercy of unfamiliar weather, their very lives were endangered by potential thieves, collapsing mines, disease, and the unknown dangers of their surroundings. Determined, they forged onward, ever keeping the prospect of unearthing the treasure in their sights.

Imagine the exhilaration, the joy, the satisfaction of finally brushing away the dirt and mud and holding those rough, golden nuggets in their own hands. All their sacrifice, time, and hard work had paid off. They had uncovered the treasure for which they had sacrificed so much and endured such hardship. Eagerly they would secure their camp, gather their nuggets, and head to the assayer's office in the nearest town in order to verify the find, authenticate their gold, and determine its value.

Upon arrival, the prospector would open the door to the assayer's office and find standing behind the counter a cautious, tidy man dressed in a crisp, clean shirt tucked into trousers held up with suspenders. Peering skeptically over the spectacles resting on the edge of his nose, he would motion to the unkempt miner to bring his 'treasure' closer for examination. Holding out his hand, he would take the nuggets and turning them over and over again, inspect them with his magnifying glass. He would then place them on the scales and jot some details in a small note pad. With very little enthusiasm, he would issue the miner his certificate of authenticity and estimated value of the find and send him on his way.

There, set in the middle of the gold rush, were two different people—one living life in the extreme seeking out the treasure he believed was hidden just below the surface of the ground; and the other keeping himself neat and clean and away from the unpredictable outcomes of mining, living each day merely to inspect another's treasure. The former could walk away knowing his endurance, labour, and hardship had brought to him unknown riches; while the latter could only imagine what it would be like to take the risk, live the adventure, and be the one to stand worn, weary, and yet strangely fulfilled on the other side of the counter.

Similarly, there seems to be two camps in the Christian world today. One is the organized local religious centre, with well-established boundaries where church life issues and 'interruptions' from the Holy Spirit are dealt with 'safely' and in accordance with the expectations of the 'majority' of the voting members. In this place, 'important doctrinal issues' are worked through with policies, protocols, and boards, and then finally come out of the 'laundering' process into neat and tidy, 'socially acceptable' programs—a program for every age. These programs meet everyone's needs, from those who feel a need to *serve* in some capacity right on to those who need to *receive* service from the religious pillars of their community. No fuss, no muss; nice and neat and clean. And on Sunday after church, the Sears catalogue family returns home to their roast beef dinner and an evening of inexpressible feelings of 'missing something' only to greet another Monday morning with an emptiness and longing in their spirits for a touch from the Master—from Jesus—their Saviour, their Redeemer, their Healer. They plod through the week, faithfully attending all the programs, while deep inside they are desperately seeking some kind of filling—although they're not sure what it is or where it should come from. After all, religion provides for all their spiritual needs. Doesn't it?

The second camp is not so clean. Here, the radical believers of Jesus Christ often worship, serve, and fight spiritual battles alone. You see, they don't fit into the neat and tidy sanitized world of most organized churches. These are the type of kingdom dwellers that, through the leading of the Holy Spirit, step out onto the narrow line drawn in the sand and grab hold of the lost. Maybe it's through public evangelism, or perhaps it's through holding a Bible study for the 'less than desirable'—those who have entered a 'church' and been ignored or discouraged from thinking they would ever belong. (They probably wouldn't call it a 'Bible study'; they would more likely call it a "Let's get real with God" meeting.) Perhaps they're the ones who, after years of disappointment and emptiness from religion, set their hearts on an independent journey with Jesus—taking Him at His Word, praying for the lost right there on the street corner, laying hands on the lame man in the department store, openly rebuking the spirit of rebellion on a child in their own home—as they unleash the power of God into the reality of their lives, their homes, their workplaces, and their community.

The Holy Spirit has got a hold of their spirit, soul, and body, and is transforming them into combat material for the Kingdom. And for those with great resolve to fearlessly and unashamedly hold up Jesus Christ before men, comes great opposition both in this world and in the spiritual realm as well. Satan cringes at the sight and smell of these radical followers of Jesus Christ and unleashes attack and assault on them, their family, their businesses, or anything they value. Demonic oppression presses down on them hoping they give up their quest for more of Jesus. They deal with rejection and ridicule from the 'church' and the world—neither of whom understand their passionate heart to shake the world for Christ. Ironically, it is through these attacks that a stronger warrior is fashioned by the hand of God.

So why do these 'outcasts' continue on? What's in it for them? I'll tell you. There is no greater joy in this world then to sense the presence and power of Jesus Christ in you; to feel the hand of the Holy Spirit press down upon your spirit with deep truths and mysteries you can't even put into words; to see human lives transformed through the power of Jesus Christ; to know you are on victory's side and experience the submission of darkness to the beautiful name of Jesus; to know that it is not all warfare all the time. There are times of great joy and dancing and singing and blessing when a battle is over. And then, the call comes again—to the front lines to take back from darkness the hold it has claimed over souls, to bring good news to the afflicted, to bind up the broken hearted, to proclaim liberty to the captives, and freedom to the prisoners. (Isaiah 61:1-2)

Are you ready to take a chance, get 'dirty,' and endure hardships and sacrifice in order to become 'rich' with treasures that moth and rust cannot corrupt? Or are you content to stand neat and tidy and safe behind the counter and merely inspect another's treasure but never being able to claim it for your own?

Given a choice, which would you choose? You have only one physical life to live here on this earth. Why not make it an extreme one?

There are great things in the kingdom that eye has not seen and ear has not heard. Are you ready to see, to hear, and to fight?

Quiet

"Be still (cease striving) and know that I am God."
(Psalm 46:10)

Quiet. Quiet your mind. Quiet the voices that move your thoughts toward things that need to be done or plans and arrangements that must be taken care of. Cease striving 'to become' or 'do' in order to hear the voice of God. Cease striving to feel Him stir your heart solely for a great cause or action or service.

Shut yourself down and ask yourself, "Do I seek to hear and feel and sense the presence of Jesus so that I and others can recognize His manifestation in me, or am I content to rest in His presence, be touched by His supernatural love, and simply abide? Am I willing to let Him accomplish what He may through me, but desire foremost His company, His presence, His love—just with me and for me?"

Can you hear your Saviour ask, "Do you search for Me and strive for My presence to spend the over-spill of My glory and power upon all the great things *you* can accomplish in My name? Or do you search and desire *Me* for the love and peace that comes from abiding in My Presence? Are you content with only Me? Are you able to live and walk an 'everyday life' on this earth with the glory and help of My power flowing through the daily tasks your life requires? Are you able to simply abide—rest—being content with Me alone?"

You know, the Father needs no one to do anything for Him. He is quite capable of managing and executing all His plans without the aid of His creations. His desire is to love us. It is our designed purpose to let Him love us without turning it into a 'manifestation'—'a visible form of service'. Believe me, when you are content to sit under the shower of His love, the whole world will be able to tell that you are 'wet'—you are 'saturated and soaked' in the love of Jesus.

So often we equate what we do with how much of 'Jesus' we 'feel' or have 'captured'. I think some of the greatest testimonies of the presence of God are found in the most unexpected places—the peaceful, quiet ways of an elderly couple sitting closely together, hand-in-hand on a park bench; the silent restful stare of a young mom carving through all the busy noise of happy, active children at a playground to drink in the joy of her little one playing in the sandbox.

This world is speeding up—quicker and quicker, faster and faster, louder and louder. Compete with it or be left behind! Not so in the kingdom. God's love is simple but more profound and overwhelming than all the hustle and bustle of the fast-talking, super-salesmen of spirituality and religion.

Come away and rest under His love. You don't need to *do* anything—that will come on its own in a natural expression of His love.

How do you know when you've come across someone who's been introduced to the sweet peace of Jesus and has visited the Kingdom? It's when you look for Jesus and you find Him in their face; and when you look into someone's face and you can't help but see Jesus there—His peace and serenity, His love, joy, and compassion.

He has a way of consuming those who have surrendered to Him—those who can let all the 'religious activities and projects and ministries' go—and simply let Him love them for no specific reason or goal or 'purpose'—but just to know Him.

When you come across someone like that, watch their life because then it's just a matter of time before the love and power of the Father will flow through their eyes, their lips, their hands, and their hearts to touch others—to infect others—with the simple but overwhelming love of God.

The Gift

❧

It was a special day. The entire family was gathered together for a day set apart — a special celebration — a day to honour their father. There was music and laughter. There were fond memories shared among the family. There was a table spread with the finest foods. It was a time of celebration.

Father was sitting in his chair — watching — taken in with satisfaction and pleasure the moments of the day. He remembered watching each of his children grow from tiny babies demanding constant attention to the invincible, strong-willed teens, right through to what were now mostly grown children setting out on their own paths, taking with them the years of love and training, encouragement and discipline given to them by a wise and loving father. A smile crossed his face as he knew each one would find their way, continuing to learn and grow as they traveled through the lessons that life inevitably holds.

One of the older children approached the father, carrying in hand a beautiful box exquisitely wrapped in the finest paper and bearing a golden bow that glittered under the light. The father reached out and accepted the gift, took it in his hands, and unwrapped its treasure—a beautiful sculpture—carved by what was truly a master craftsman. The family 'ooed and awed' and complimented the son on his fine work and worthiness of the gift. The father set the gift aside and took the child—although grown—onto his lap and embraced him warmly and whispered, "Thank you, son. You have given me a beautiful gift. I see your heart in this gift. I love you too."

A short time later, another child made his way to the father carefully carrying a small package wrapped in brown paper and tied so very meticulously with a piece of string. The family looked on, wondering whatever could be in such a plain package. The father opened the gift and a smile crossed his face. He held in his hands a small wooden carving with jagged edges and dotted with nicks and gouges. The family smiled acceptingly. The father set the gift aside his chair and opened his arms to receive the child onto his lap, embraced him warmly, and whispered, "Thank you, my child. You have given me a beautiful gift. I see your heart in this gift and I love you too."

The day continued to pass with stories and memories shared among the family. Nearing the end of the celebration, a small child approached the father, clutching in his tight fist a crumpled piece of paper wrapped around a small item. He was awkward and shy, and hesitated about bringing his treasure to his father. The family looked on, not paying much notice to the child, but watching with anticipation the father's reaction. Silence spread over the room as the young boy made his way to the father's chair. Hands shaking and with a tremor in his voice, he held out his crumpled paper wad to the father and in a shy, quiet whisper said, "I made something for you, Daddy." The father gently took the gift and gingerly unwrapped it. He carefully held in his hand a small stone with a simple heart painted on the side and the words, "I love you" scratched along the bottom. The family awkwardly smiled, glanced at each other, and shifted uneasily in their seats. A smile crossed the father's face and a small tear was making its way down his cheek. He lay the gift aside and opened his arms wide, beckoning the wee child to come onto his lap. The child eagerly crawled up and was locked in a warm embrace. The father whispered, "Thank you, my little one. You have given me a beautiful gift. I see your heart in this gift, and I love you, too."

The family didn't know quite what to do next. Slowly conversations resumed and the day progressed along uneventfully. One by one, people left the cele-bration, each carrying inside them questions about the day. It didn't make sense. Father whispered the same thing to each one who brought a gift. Didn't he notice the fine sculpture, the rough wooden carving, or the little painted stone?

Yes. He noticed the gifts and accepted and was honoured by each, but it was the heart of the giver that touched him most.

The kingdom is a funny place where things are not the way they are here in our world—a world infused with human-laden perceptions of acceptable and unacceptable, worthy and unworthy. So many of us see only with our human eyes and sense only with our human hearts, both of which are often clouded with perfectionism and comparison.

It is the way of the kingdom to honour—as our Father does—those who may bring even the smallest and unrefined gifts. Too often, those who are permitted and encouraged to present their gifts to the heavenly Father are those who have humanly refined their talent in such a way that the heart is shut out and it is merely a performance or presentation of excellence. There is no room for the Holy Spirit to move within such 'control'. There is no room for a heart to express an impromptu impulse of love and adoration to our Saviour, our God. Where have we taken worship so that we are no longer free to display our hearts through our gifts, regardless of how refined or finished or perfected they might be?

What have we allowed to happen as we scorn or criticize, reject or condemn those who dare bring an unrefined crumpled wad of a gift to the Father—all the while crippling, stifling, and maiming little ones in the body of Christ?

We can never bring human perfection in performance to the Father because we will not be perfect in this life; BUT, we can bring a heart of pure love and adoration to worship the One who Is and let the expression of our heart transport our love to His heart. Perfect love casts out all fear—fear of judgement, criticism, rejection, or condemnation.

He is perfect love. He knows what your heart can't fully express humanly, but He sees what you long to bring to Him—as a little child—undaunted by those around you, motivated out of love for Him, not caring of appearances but totally consumed in His full acceptance and unconditional love.

Do not be afraid to show your heart to the Father. Yes, be prepared for human skepticism and rejection, but know your Father accepts your gift and sees your heart; and you will be strengthened because you have let loose your heart to flow to His and His to you.

Do you want to live as one in the kingdom? Then encourage others to bring their gifts to the Father. Give honour to even the littlest one who brings to the Father a small gift—a display of heart worship to the King—regardless of how well it manifests itself within our flawed human framework of acceptability. Humble yourself. Let all striving to be noticed by the Father fall away. He sees you—He sees everyone. No one goes unnoticed. Make a way for the faltering ones with small, untidy gifts, as well as stronger ones with eloquent and refined offerings to come into the

Father's presence. Encourage them to bring what they have in their hearts to God—a spiritual service of worship.

It is when we understand and grasp the magnitude of the Father's heart that we will cease to hinder others in order to get the Father's attention through *our* acts of worship. We will then move in unison as a body—each a valuable member of a beautiful orchestra—sometimes playing together, sometimes a solo, but all worthy and honourable vessels bringing the beauty of pure love and worship to the Holy One who alone is worthy of glory, honour, and praise.

"But Jesus said, 'Let the children alone, and do not hinder them from coming to Me; for the kingdom of heaven belongs to such as these.'" (Matthew 19:14)

The Road Less Traveled

There is nothing that compares with the thrill and deep-seated drive to pursue the Most High when one's heart and soul has been awakened to the purpose He has placed within you.

This awakening can come to you either through revelation and insight from the Holy Spirit, or perhaps He has spoken to you through a prophetic word from another. Regardless of how He chooses to reveal His plan for you, it is one of the most empowering moments — to know God has put His 'stamp' on you — chosen you — to manifest His glory and power in some amazing way.

This fact alone can keep a person on a spiritual high for some time, catapulting you into a deeper relationship with your Heavenly Father.

Then slowly, gradually, and through time, the passion and fire seem to lessen. It may even turn to a few embers hidden under the darkened remains of charcoal that were once alive and glowing with fire, passion, and power.

Why would God give such a revelation and then appear to sit back and watch as the flames lessen and smoke starts to curl from the once-burning embers that now are little more than ashes?

Why doesn't He keep the flame going? Why do the doors of ministry not open while you're *hot* for Him? Why, when you look around at the workings of God in others, does it seem they're on their way and you've been left to live out your days in a 'what could have been' existence?

Perhaps you console yourself by thinking, "I've once felt a burning for the Lord, but now I'll just be content to exist and plod along through this life, live as close to normalcy as possible, and keep my spiritual life down to an unthreatening and complacent stroll through my days on earth."

So how does one stop the spiral into self-pity, resolution to a mundane relationship with God, and giving up on your divine deposit of purpose?

Tough questions and a harsh kingdom reality—until you look at it a different way—maybe rising above this immediate moment to look over the span of your years—previous, present, and future—and to return to the heroes of our faith that have been recorded in the best history record ever—the Word of God—to use as a guide, a template, a faithful witness to the love and wisdom of our Creator.

When your heart and soul have been awakened to God's purpose for you, and your whole being begins to vibrate with energy, enthusiasm, and vision for your Saviour and His work, you have just entered a road—a path—where you will be strengthened, tested, taught, and refined.

All start out on the road together, anticipating the day when everyone recognizes your anointing—the mighty hand of an awesome God on you. Soon, though, the path is not as crowded. Some have left the path because darkness—the enemy—has come and lured them away from their calling with the things of this world.

Others have become weary and impatient and have chosen the faster track that veers from the path as a fork in the road—the path that appears to offer them opportunity and exposure quickly, ushering them speedily into their 'calling'. It's almost like saying, "If I can't operate in the power of God soon, I'll just make my own way. I'll arrange my own circumstances. Rub shoulders with the right people and talk the talk that will take me to where I feel God calling me. I'll put myself in the place where others will see His anointing on me."

Sure, God's power may manifest through that person. Others are reached, touched, saved, and even healed. But soon, maybe a few years, their momentum does not originate from the Saviour. The catalyst for ministry becomes 'their ministry'—their books, their tapes, their seminars, their visions, their conferences—all speeding up quickly—all consuming—to ensure their place in the 'spiritual giants wall of fame' is secure and 'locked in' in the minds of those significant throughout the world.

Many of these well-meaning warriors soon succumb to temptation, compromise, or physical and spiritual exhaustion. Their ministry can be likened to a no-name battery. It does give enough juice to get the immediate job done, to make the machine run; but it peters out quickly. It couldn't make it to completion.

What's next? Either they disappear into obscurity or they push themselves through their ministry, continuing to turn out tapes and books and seminars. Meanwhile the real power of God has been substituted—replaced—for the 'power of expectancy' from those following what was once a spiritual superstar.

Do you want to be a superstar?

There is another road that is traveled less frequently and less noticeable, however. It is a road that is sometimes enshrouded in a fog. You can't see behind or before you—just the step you take—one at a time. This road is quiet at times and sometimes lonely. On this path, the Spirit of God reveals Himself in quietness. At other times, He is evident through an encounter with just one individual you happen to see at the side of the road, stepping out of the fog. You encourage them, pray for them, heal them — all through Jesus' name — and then continue on.

What's happening on this less-trodden path while those who took the fast lane are busy, busy, busy with kingdom work?

God is busy, busy, busy with you. Patience requires strength. Patience, endurance, and faithfulness is busy, busy work. The Spirit of God is building you in these quiet times. Be encouraged and let Him do what He does best — making you into His image — a reflection of holy strength, holy endurance and faithfulness, and holy power from on High.

When the road begins to brighten, the way becomes clearer, and the fog lifts, you turn around and see behind you the many, many people you touched with God's hand of love as you walked along — steadily and faithfully — even when it seemed you were all alone. The thousands of ones you touched may not have been gathered together under one roof in a convention centre offering applause or standing in awe of how God manifested Himself through you, but they will stand together before God. Your faithfulness has been used to bring them closer to the Most High.

Will you ever enter into the public arena—into a 'ministry' that others recognize—where crowds gather to see the glory of God descend on you and you minister in marvelous ways— where people want your books, and tapes, and CD's?

Perhaps—and perhaps not.

Keep walking along the lonely road—the quiet, long road—where the Potter's hand is forming you into a solid vessel—not easily broken—not easily swayed—able to hold securely and without leaking and cracking, all that God pours into you—able to withstand pressure from without—pressure to produce results, pressure to 'go big' into ministry before God directs you to, pressure to perform without power.

I'll leave you with a question. Do you pursue God because of what you think He'll do through you, or do you pursue God because you love Him?

Would you pursue the Father to the same extent and with the same passion if you knew your life would be spent ministering one-on-one in daily encounters appointed by God with men, women, and children who would forget your name but not your Saviour? If the answer is 'yes,' you are a worthy vessel. Hold on steady to the Saviour's hand through the high energy of active service and down those quiet, foggy roads with just Him and you.

Remain faithful as He is faithful.

BATTLE SCARS

Wartime in the Kingdom

It's wartime in the kingdom of God. The sound of the shofar thunders through the kingdom—that invisible world—that spiritual world—where forces of darkness hurl flaming missiles to cripple, maim, and scar those in the Light. Where children of Light take up their weapons and without fear or reservation slice the enemy to pieces and trample on him till he rises no more.

Are the only fierce and mighty warriors of the kingdom of God those who are in the public eye, those who stand tall behind a pulpit week after week, evoking awe and reverence from those in the pew? Are the warriors only those who sacrifice earthly comforts to preach Christ to the poorer nations, bringing fantastic stories of the unbelievable back to those who cannot go? Perhaps the only fierce and mighty warriors are those who travel the globe holding seminars and conferences, building and equipping the body, telling of the 'fantastic,' the 'supernatural' revelations, and amazing manifestations of God occurring in their ministry.

It is true. Those are truly mighty men and women of God who battle the darkness to hold forth the Word of Life and Jesus Christ. We need warriors like that today more than ever.

Does that mean you and I are less than warriors? Maybe we believe we are merely weekend warriors who gather together and feel a little heat from the presence of God as the 'full time fighters' for the kingdom bring forth the message. We pray and prophesy and are prophesied over and then go home to our chicken dinner and leave the rest of the battle to the full time fighters.

For some, that is all they desire; and that is all they receive.

For 'disciples'—those who follow Jesus Christ and understand that to do so wholly will mean persecution and trial—it is not enough. We crave to belong in the front lines of battle. We know the power and authority of Jesus Christ. We know we are more than conquerors. We desire the power of the Holy Spirit to course through every fiber of our being. We desire to see the Holy Spirit touch the lives of the redeemed in order to bring restoration and healing; to touch the hearts of the lost so as to bring redemption and freedom from the choking clutch of Satan's grip around their necks.

How do we reconcile our desire to be a warrior in the Kingdom with our lives—the everyday life—where we go to work, where we send our kids to school, where we pump gas, stock shelves, shuffle papers, tend to the sick, sell insurance, or make supper, wash clothes, and do dishes?

Don't be deceived by the lie of Satan that you are not useful to the Most High simply because you are not on the 'front lines' or because you may not be in 'full time' ministry (and be careful—it may come for you when you least expect it).

The kingdom of darkness envelops this world. It doesn't just touch down on the missionaries, pastors, healers, or full time conference speakers. It reaches its bony claws down into your life—your family, your neighbours, your co-workers—attempting to strangle the Life from you; trying to extinguish your Light with the dark, heavy breath of lies spoken into your soul—the lies that you are forgotten and mediocre and unimportant to the kingdom.

Ask the Holy Spirit to open your eyes. Ask Jesus Christ to forgive you for looking at everyone else; for comparing yourself to the man or woman in the pew ahead of you, or the pastor or missionary or the televangelist. Ask the Spirit of Truth to put blinders on you to stop you from looking around and comparing, and to increase your spiritual vision—your Kingdom perception—to see how the dark spiritual realm reaches deep into our everyday encounters, thoughts, and feelings to warp our minds and souls and put a wedge between our spirit and the Spirit of God—to make us and keep us ineffective for God.

Wake up, O sleeper, and redeem the time! Quit drumming your fingers, waiting for the 'big stuff' everyone says that kingdom warfare is all about, and look for the crack where darkness is silently slipping in and spoiling what belongs to the children of Light while we wait for the 'bigger and better' to come along.

Every disciple of Jesus Christ **is** a full time warrior. Don your armour and be vigilant for the devil is as a roaring lion seeking to devour anyone he can.

There is no small battle in the kingdom of God. In fact, many unseen battles—those tearful prayers for salvation and healing, protection and direction for family, friends and whomever the Holy Spirit brings into your mind or life—are often the battles that make a difference between life and death.

These battles often are catalytic. They cause a ripple effect in the kingdom. Your seemingly small and irrelevant warfare today—that quick prayer or that instant rebuke of the enemy as soon as you recognize his presence—has a lasting impact on eternity and on behalf of those for whom you wage war.

Does attack come to the unseen warrior as greatly as the public one? Yes, and sometimes more so because it is the faithfulness of the foot soldiers marching onward step by step, mile by mile, day after day, and year after year, in rain and cold and hunger, that effectively takes back the land from the hand of Satan and returns it to the rightful owner—the Creator—the King of Kings and Lord of Lords—and His heirs—that's you and me!

Discouragement, self-pity, feelings of worthlessness and unimportance—these will be your enemies, and these are often fought alone—just you and them on a desolate secret battlefield—the battlefield of your inner man—your secret thoughts and feelings. Be on guard! When you recognize these lies be sure you've stepped on some toes from the darkness. Strengthen yourself with the Word of God, the blood of Jesus, and the Spirit of Truth. Pick up your sword and trample them down again and again as you march steadily onward, pushing back the forces of darkness to make room for the kingdom of Light and Love—the Kingdom of God.

Then, one day our King will come and you will stand shoulder to shoulder in the front line along with all the rest—all the warriors that faithfully battled for their King: the powerful healers, the mighty evangelists, the faithful little old lady from church, the tired parents who prayerfully fought for the souls of their children, and the little one who prayed for his mother and father.

Loneliness

There are different kinds of loneliness. Some are a result of sinful choices on our part that place a wedge between ourselves and fellowship with the Holy Spirit. Until we seek repentance and turn from our sinful ways, then is our communion restored and we once again fall into the sweet, loving embrace of our Father.

Another type of loneliness may also cover our mind and spirit as a result of our own plans and expectations that go unmet. This may happen either through the action or inaction of another person, or when our expectations and hopes of what the Father has promised to do through us may not be unfolding in the time or manner we desired or expected.

Unmet expectations can cause us to draw away from loved ones and even from our heavenly Father. Mostly it is an opportunity jumped upon by dark forces to separate you— alienate you—through hurt, disappointment, and discouragement. It can weed you out much like a wounded or sick lamb falls behind the flock and is easy prey for the wolves.

Our own thinking cascades into a torrent of presuppositions and conclusions we draw in our own mind, spurred on by self-pity, hurt, and bitterness. We, in effect, build a wall around us that, if left in place, will close us in and effectually close us down. Our emotions, our thoughts, our passions, and our communion with the Father all become like those of a robot—just going through the motions of existence and habit.

Under it all, dark forces are silently and steadily eating away at your spirit like termites taking small pieces of what used to be desire, passion, and purpose fueled by love for the Most High. If you or a loved one does not recognize this process, it can lead to a precious soul living only a life of resignation to bare existence.

Discouragement and disappointment with God are red flags of opportunity for dark forces to come and whisk you off to an island in the middle of nowhere, where you are left to your own reasoning and feelings of abandonment, forever fueled by self-pity and misconceptions of God's true character and purpose for your existence.

You must wake up! Shake and stir up your soul—your mind—your heart—to realize our ways and plans and times are not always the same as our Father's. Return to His Word. Take Him at His Word that He will not leave undone a work He has begun.

There is another description of loneliness that needs to be identified. Often when you have passed through the loneliness due to unmet expectations, you may end up here.

This loneliness is a 'quietness of spirit'. You are no longer disappointed or bitter towards God for not 'delivering' on your desired expectations of His purpose for you. You have passed through those fleshly feelings and have now reckoned yourself with God's intrinsic faithfulness, His promises, and His perfect plan for you—regardless of what you think or desire.

It seems as if your flesh is dead. You go through each day performing the tasks, duties, and responsibilities that keep your life moving onward—like gears in a machine that continue to turn unhindered.

Yet, something is different. Underneath—deep in your spirit—there is peace. There is a knowing that the Potter is working, removing unneeded pieces of clay, adding shape and form to the remainder, molding and plying and guiding His hands over the supple clay to fashion it into His purpose—into His image.

At times, your spirit cries out to the Father for drops of His presence to stir your soul and flesh again—like rain on parched ground. You long for the days before when your body, soul, and spirit would rise up to Him and be consumed in His glory and presence. When your flesh felt the heaviness of His Spirit and you could hardly move, and your mind was empty while He filled your soul and spirit with inexpressible mysteries and awareness of His glory. A time where a flood of the heavenly language would pour from your lips and tears of love and adoration would stream from your eyes as you surrendered to the Spirit in unutterable groanings. To again read from the Words of Life and have the Holy Spirit guide the revelation—the truth of the Word—so deep within your very fiber that it took time for your mind and flesh to be able to articulate—to interpret—the revelation—the message.

These are like cool rain drops—like waterfalls of blessing—to a heart that loves and longs for the Father. But there is more, especially for those that are not content with a containable God—a God so many keep in a box. There is so much more for those who want to see Him unhindered to consume their life—their world. There is this time of 'aloneness' when the heavens don't open with raindrops to fall upon your face.

It's deeper right now. It's quiet now—at this time. What Father would not continue to nurture His child—even in times of refining and molding? For deep, deep underground—deep in the spirit—there is a River that flows—the River of Life that waters the spirit from underneath the surface. The River which, when you stretch your roots into its flow, will infuse you with life and strength, understanding, and unshakeability in this time—the River that brings pure sustenance to the soul and spirit. Jeremiah talks of a tree which when the drought comes will not be anxious but will continue to yield fruit. Take heart. Let the underground river nurture you in this quietness. Outwardly you may appear like a tree in the throws of winter—lifeless, naked of any signs of life and colour and vitality, barren against the sky—but deep within your spirit, 'roots' are absorbing life-giving nutrients from the Giver of Life—the River of Life. The deeper the roots, the more stable the tree. Winter winds may blow and storms of ice and snow may whirl about, but the tree still remains after the storm—all intact—and deep below, the roots continue to anchor you through it all.

When you recognize this place in your journey with the Father, you then can rest and let the Father, the Master Creator, continue to create in you—to make and refine you. You can feel the fruit coming forth as you wait, all the while drawing on the River of Life.

What fruit? The fruit of the Spirit—pure fruit—because your flesh is DEAD. You have no energy, desire, or will to put on the signs of godliness in your own strength. In this place, the fruit is all from the

Spirit. Let it flow out of you. Let Him work out of you while the hand of God continues to work in you. Let love, joy, peace, patience, kindness, goodness, faithfulness, gentleness, and self control run through you while you wait for the work to be accomplished.

You know and I know the work will be completed to perfection only upon our King's return. But take heart; this 'alone' time will pass. In the meantime, please keep with you the secret of the underground River that always flows with life-giving water that nourishes and replenishes your innermost being which may appear at this moment in time to be barren and dormant. Wherever the hand of the Father guides you, let the Spirit bring forth the fruit that is needed for that moment, for all we truly have is this moment to be a reflection of our Father.

Your life will no longer be the same now because it doesn't matter what you feel or do. You realize that it doesn't matter if you feel His overwhelming presence at this moment or if your flesh and soul and spirit are in a quiet place because His Spirit is still within you. You realize that it doesn't matter if you are ministering publicly and great signs and wonders are taking place or if you simply whisper a word of love and encouragement to someone sitting alone on a park bench because His Spirit is still within you. You realize it doesn't matter about your flesh anymore. You are not here for what you can 'feel' and 'experience'. You are here as an ambassador, as a representative, as 'fruit' of the Spirit that dwells within you.

The more He has of us, the less we have of ourselves. And that means less striving and more peace, less anxiety and worry and more faith and trust, less disappointment and anger and more joy and patience and understanding.

It is all about Him. What part of Himself does He desire to reveal through you—His chosen vessel—right now—today?

Discouragement

I believe words have colours. Not just one colour to represent its meaning but many shades of colours to represent the many facets or depths of a word.

Discouragement is such a word with many shades or degrees. If I were to colour it, I would choose black with all its variations. Some discouragement is but a tinge of gray that is quickly brushed away with an encouraging word from a friend or remembering your value and significance to the Father. Other discouragement may be a little more intense with shades of heavy, steel gray mingled with dark streaks of black. It may take more time and the healing touch of the Master to wash away this discouragement and bring up the hidden colours of joy and peace that lay beneath. The darkest colour of discouragement is black for when it enshrouds you in its heavy cloak it is as if there is no ray of light that could ever penetrate its depth. Your very life and breath seem laboured under its seemingly unending heaviness while remembrances of lighter days filled with the bright yellows, reds, blues, and greens of your life seem so far away and far beyond your grasp.

With this heaviness, there is also a pain which accompanies discouragement that is often felt deep within but seldom able to be expressed with words. The pain of discouragement is often accompanied by the ache of loneliness and sense of abandonment, mingled with the sting of self-pity. What a fine collection—one only capable of being specially proportioned by the hands of the thief himself. You know—the one who comes to steal and kill and destroy.

Regardless of your previous experiences with God, your faith, or your future dreams, discouragement has the potential of stopping one dead in their tracks, crippling them of moving ahead—even a small bit—with the tiniest amount of hope, snuffing out and dulling any memory of the past blessing and closeness you felt from the Father, and bringing all senses and desires for today to a deadening standstill.

What brings on this shroud of discouragement?

There may be a number of contributing factors or many different circumstances to initiate the spiral downward.

One seems to be when you have experienced a deepening of faith or a special closeness or revelation of the character of Jesus. It's as if darkness lingers in the wings, waiting to snatch from you the treasure your Father has given.

This spirit of darkness is not unlike a bully who waits outside the candy store to spring upon a little one who has just bought a bag of penny candy with the quarter given to him by his father for no reason other than just to show his love for his child.

The little boy's candy is ripped from his hands and the bully stuffs it into his mouth and devours it. He laughs at the little one and pushes him onto the ground. Laughing and mocking, he says, "Where's your daddy now? See, you're all by yourself. Nobody's coming to help you. You can't do anything about it. In fact, I bet your dad doesn't even care. He'll probably just laugh when you tell him what happened. Your dad's going to be really angry at you because you lost your candy and wasted his money. He doesn't care about you, you know. He's forgotten you even went to the store. Just remember—I'll be here the next time you get a little hand out from your 'daddy,' and I'll take that one too!"

The little fellow is unable to comprehend this atrocity in his mind. He was dwelling on the blessing from his father and anticipating the look of joy on his dad's face when he would show him the bag of treats they would share together. He cannot fathom the cruelty of such a being. He just stands there, not knowing where to turn, unable to grasp what has happened not only to his candy—his blessing—but to his feelings of joy and blessedness. Tears stream down the little boy's face and uncontrollable sobbing shakes his little body.

When asked to explain his tears to a passerby, he can hardly put into words the devastation brought to his heart. It is inexpressible—too deep for such a little one to articulate—so many different places where the blow has wounded.

On one hand, he cries at the loss of his candy—the tangible evidence of his father's blessing and love—something that brought the depth of the father's love into the understandable realm of the child. On the other hand, it is the realization of the insidious depravity and darkness that constantly lurks behind the corners to snatch away any joy from another. As well, the pain of that aching feeling of a lost moment spent together with his dad as he was eagerly looking forward to crawling up into his father's lap to share his candy with him.

The little boy has choices to make.

He can stand there and cry and remain in that moment for however long he chooses; or he can wipe his tears, make his way home without his candy, knowing that the bully can steal his candy but he can't take his father's love away from him. "My father has lots of quarters to spend on me," he tells himself. And his father will again—at another time—press a quarter into his little hand and send him on his way to the store.

But most of all, the little boy just wants to run into the embrace of his dad, tell him how much it hurt to lose his candy, and feel the love and protection from the strong arms of his father who holds him tight. He hears his father say, "It's o.k. It's not the quarters or the candy that matter. What matters is that you know where to run when the bully tries to steal your treasure. I have all kinds of treasures for you, my little one. Don't fear of losing the ones you hold in your hand for the ones that can't be stolen are held in your heart."

The little boy leans against the father's chest, held closely by his strong, warm arms. He hears the steady, strong heartbeat of his father. It's good here. He rests for a while as his father wipes his tears from his face and whispers in his ear. The boy takes a deep breath, scrambles off his lap, and is ready again to face the world.

Discouragement is a dark colour that at times seems to enshroud us like mourning clothes worn at a wake. Hold tight to the Father as the clouds of discouragement swirl around. They may slow you down, but if your heart belongs to Jesus you know that deep inside you a root of faith is steadily anchoring you and will keep you tethered to the Father. Summon up the strength to walk against the storm. Brave the downpour and walk by faith, not by feeling.

Continue to do those things God has placed in your heart. Love Him and praise Him regardless of your feelings. Love your husband or your wife. Love your children. Minister to others out of your pain because God's strength is made known in your weakness.

The clouds will pass and the storm will calm, and you will once again see clearly the face of Jesus—the One whom you love—and your faith will be deepened because of this storm.

Deepened and strengthened.

Yes, storms will come again and when you recognize the signs—the clouds, the winds, the temperature change—brace yourself with the truth—the truth that the Father promised never to leave you, and because He is at your right hand, you will not be shaken.

The Bench Warmer

The bench was filled with anxious, squirming little ones who were so eager to get in and play the game. For one little boy, the past days and weeks and months were filled with practicing whenever and wherever he had a chance.

He met faithfully with the team once a week for group practices, but that wasn't enough for him. He would run into his backyard after school and practice sliding into first base. Then he would jump up, dust off his pants, and take a running dive into second base. Again, he would jump to his feet, straighten his cap, and make the dash to his imaginary third base. Crouched over with hands on his knees, he would look around as if waiting for the signal. With a burst, he would tear off third and make the grandest slide into home. Throwing his cap into the air and waving his arms, he would run around the plate and cheer. You would think this young fellow was playing in the big leagues. His mom, with a smile on her face, would open the patio door and call her little all-star in for supper.

Days passed much similar to this one. Sometimes the little boy would be seen with a bucket of balls in an empty field. One after another, he would toss a ball into the air and strike at it with all his might. Sometimes he would recruit a neighbour and would have them throw sliders, curve balls, and fly balls over and over until the sun began to set and it became too dark to see the incoming balls. It wasn't a surprise to see the little one asleep in his uniform, oftentimes with the rule book lying open upon his chest. He lived and breathed the game. It was his reason for being, and thoughts of the game filled his every waking moment. It was his passion, his purpose—all that really seemed to matter in this little one's world.

Finally the big day arrived—the day they had all been waiting for—especially this little one. Today was the day of the big game. The little boy was up early, dressed, and ready to go in lots of time. He arrived at the field and was eagerly greeted by the coach and the rest of the team. Chatter filled the dug out as plans were being made for strategy and line up. Crowds soon filled the bleachers and the game was about to begin.

The first line up was set and the players took their place. It was exciting for the little boy to watch. He could hardly wait for his turn to bat. "Batter up," yelled the coach, and the next player would run onto the plate and take their position.

Time after time, the coach would call for the next batter. Time after time, the little boy would glance down the bench to see if he was any closer to being called up to action. "When will I get to go up and take my turn?" thought the little boy. "Why hasn't the coach called on me? He knows I've been practicing. He knows how much I've waited for this day. He knows that I haven't missed even one practice. Why is he just leaving me to sit here on this bench when all the other players have been called out?" The little one seemed to lose his enthusiasm for the game now and it seemed to just drag on and on with little hope in sight for him to ever be called up to bat.

Discouragement, frustration, and anger began to creep over him like a dark, foreboding shadow. With shoulders slumped, hat in his hand, he kept his eyes on the ground, kicking away at the small stones and dust, while thoughts of hurt and unfairness started to twist in his heart and mind.

All his dedication and hard work were for nothing. Here it was the big day and he was the only one not called on to help bring the team to victory. Nobody seemed to even notice him. "I might as well be invisible—nobody needs me anyway," a voice rang over and over again in his mind. "Why am I wasting my time here? They don't need me. They don't care. I should just go hang out with the guys at the concession stand. At least they seem to be enjoying themselves."

The little boy glanced over to the booth and noticed a group of boys he knew. They were laughing and enjoying the hotdogs, pop, and snacks available at the stand. He couldn't help but keep glancing their way. They seemed to be having all the fun today.

"I might as well go join them. The coach hasn't called on me yet anyway and if he does, I'll still be able to hear him," thought the boy. Slipping off the bench and sliding through the wire fence to the food booth, the little boy joined up with the group of boys. With his back turned to the game, he entered into their fun and borrowed some money for a hotdog and pop. "I don't need them anyway—it was just a big waste of time. They are doing fine without me," he consoled himself.

Suddenly, he heard a familiar voice shouting over the crowd. Again and again the voice called his name. It was the coach! He was calling for him. "Why now? Why after most of the game was done would he call for me now?" The little boy dropped his hotdog and pop and scrambled back through the wire fence and ran up to the coach. "Here I am, Coach," he gasped as he tucked in his shirt and quickly adjusted his cap. "Where were you, son?" asked the coach. "I was calling for you."

"I didn't think you needed me or cared if I played today so I went off to the concession stand to get a treat and hang out with some friends," the little boy mumbled with his head down as he kicked his shoe into the soft dirt.

"What do you mean 'I didn't need you'?" questioned the Coach. "Just because you weren't called to play when all the others were doesn't mean you aren't necessary to the team. Everyone has a part to play in the game. There is a time for each player to use his skills to help bring us the victory. Each player brings something different to the game, and it is my place to call on the skill needed for a particular time. When you are not called, it is your job to cheer on the team that's out in the field and encourage them to keep going. I called you last because I have been watching you. We are in a tough position right now, and we need a pinch hitter who has the strength to hit a home run and the speed to make it around the bases. I know you've been faithfully practicing all the skills I've taught you, and I've seen you practicing for hours by yourself in the field. It is your time to come and work with us to bring the team to victory."

The little boy hung his head in shame, feeling so sorry for his self-pity and discouragement that almost cost the team to forfeit the game. The coach put his arm around the little boy's shoulder and said, "Now, get out there and do what I've trained you to do. It is your time to prove yourself."

The little boy picked up his bat and took a couple of practice swings. He took a deep breath and held his head up high, eyed the pitcher, assessed the layout of the field, and had already figured out just where to land that ball. Sure enough, he hit the ball into the left outfield and he started to race around the bases. Pulling up to third, he took a glance around and realized he just might be able to make it home. With determination to prove his worthiness to the coach, he mustered all his strength and tore to home plate. He slipped into a slide and reaching his toe toward the plate, just managed to touch it before the ball hit the catcher's mitt.

You know, sometimes we are like that little boy in the game. We anticipate the day we are called to serve the Most High. We practice what we will say, what we will do, and how things will turn out. Then when that day finally comes, we are often hit with a myriad of feelings—discouragement, jealousy, anger, hurt, self-pity—as we feel that we didn't get to participate the way we had thought.

It is so difficult because our love for the Most High is so real and so intense that there is nothing we would not do for Him. Our faith in His power and possibilities for the impossible is great, and we expect to see His glory cut through the heavens and touch down right there before us. Then when it doesn't happen the way we think or, even worse, if we seem to have been left out of the 'play,' we take our ball and bat and go home to sulk in the loneliness and darkness of our own self-defeating thoughts.

Darkness loves it. Satan and his cohorts wait for moments like this when trained and passionate warriors get their feelings hurt and run home to hide. There they can do their best work—while you're hiding in the dark and entertaining thoughts that are not true and holy and pure. There they can whittle away at your devotion and faith in the Faithful One and get you to set your eyes on the 'candy booth' they operate. They seduce you to come to the concession stand, try out the treats, and hang out with the gang that's having all the fun and where you're sure to be accepted.

In the meantime, a call comes for you to step into action and but you have let your armour slip off and have let the weapons rust, thinking the Most High has lots of other warriors to call on and He doesn't really need you anyway.

Yes, the Most High has lots of other warriors He has trained to fight in battle. Yes, the Most High doesn't really 'need' anyone to do His work. But what you may not understand is that He delights in training all warriors—great and small alike—and to see them pick up their weapons when called and to see them cheer and encourage the ones on the battle-field while they are still in the wings waiting for the call forward. The Most High delights in using vessels made of clay because then the glory must go to Him because on our own, we are weak and unable to run the bases, dodge the incoming balls, and slide victoriously into Home.

Don't be discouraged if the Most High has taken you aside, trained you in battle, given you a purpose deep in your spirit to do His work, and yet has seemed to let you sit on the bench and simply observe the game others are playing. He is faithful to bring everything He has placed in you to pass. He will call you out of the dug-out when He is ready.

Are you willing to wait and to cheer on the team as they fight the good fight?

Are you willing to simply keep your eyes on the game and to offer advice and encouragement to those in the field?

Are you willing to keep your spiritual eyes on the game and not on the distractions that come when the scent of self-pity and discouragement waft pass you and entice you to leave the bench?

Are you willing to wait?

I hope you are because it is often when one leaves the bench, that the call comes from the Captain to pick up your weapon and head out onto the field.

Will He find you ready?

Time and Season Demons

The new year is barely four weeks along as this is written and for many of us we have taken down the calendars from last year and hung new ones in their place. We look forward to the fresh, new pictures each month for the next year.

There is, without doubt, in each home one calendar set apart from the rest. The others hang silently in their designated spots to add a colourful, homey touch to a room or to serve as a quick reminder of the day and month.

The one, though, that is reserved for its unique task is quite different. This calendar is laid open upon the table and each month is carefully examined and given appropriate attention. Methodically, we flip to the first month and carefully note the special days that are unique to our lives. It could be a birthday or perhaps an anniversary. Regardless, we continue to meticulously flip through month by month being so very careful not to overlook that special someone or that significant date.

It's strange how just filling in the calendar with names can bring alive to our memory the many other times in years gone by where we may have celebrated someone's birth or marriage or special event.

There are some events that don't make it to the calendar we hang in that prominent place in our homes. These events may not be so pleasant. In fact, they may stir up for us feelings, thoughts, and events we'd rather not acknowledge. Everyone can attest to this. Flipping through month by month perhaps you become saddened when coming to April when you realize that was the month your mom passed away. Perhaps it's the loss of a child, or a divorce, or an accident or illness that claimed a family member or maybe a dear friend. Perhaps a particular day or month or season brings back remembrances of a very difficult time for you.

It is strange that as we anticipate the new year ahead, we undoubtedly are reminded of the pain of the past that seems to be forever clocked into our being and is set loose to ring through us as the page of the calendar flips over once again.

Sometimes there are events in our life that have brought us to a low spot—a spot where we thought we'd never rise from again. It is a lonely spot where we feel pain that we can solely bare ourselves—a place in which it seems that everyone around us is completely oblivious to our struggle deep within and the silent tears shed in the dark and quiet places. There are those events that life brings along that usher in sorrow and loss, and our grief at times seems to sweep us to an island where we struggle with it alone until the passing of time slowly eases the ache buried so deeply within.

No one is immune to these times. No one can walk this earth without feeling the effects of sin and death. And somehow, we pass through these desert places and travel on through the days, weeks, and months as the emotional, mental, and spiritual impact lessens, and life covers us over like a gentle tide that ushers in the waves and covers the stones along the sandy shore.

As time passes and healing occurs, it becomes easier to carry on. The dips of sorrow are farther apart now, and we begin to pick up our pace once more as we walk through our daily tasks that keep life marching onward.

Then, perhaps after several months, we hit a low. It seems to have come out of nowhere. We are unable to connect it to any specific event at the time. We try to rationalize it with excuses such as a virus, hormonal challenges, being run down from work, or just simply needing a break from the routine. All our attempts at finding the source of our sorrow fail, and we are left wondering if we are ever going to be able to climb out of the pit of sadness and despair.

Why do these times come? Why, if we have dealt with a specific sin in the past, does God allow old remembrances to rear their ugly heads? Why, when we have walked through the five stages of a grief counseling course, does sorrow over a loss of a loved one through death or divorce engulf us with the same relentless fury as if it had just occurred? Why, if we've given everything over to God and His healing has lifted us from the pit, do we suddenly find ourselves down in the mire once again?

I think sometimes that we fail to remember we have an adversary that roams around looking for someone to devour—to kill, to destroy, or to steal away their peace, forgiveness, and healing. Satan and his demons have walked this earth for centuries and have gathered boundless information on those he hates the most—those unbelievably precious creations made in the image of the Most High Himself. The forces of darkness have watched, listened to, and studied humanity with one purpose in mind—namely to kill, steal and destroy.

Is it any wonder that after years and years of mapping human behaviour, they developed a keen awareness that we humans live according to cycles? I'm talking about seasons and times. We mark our calendars and keep track of events, and they are all stored deep within our subconscious—locked in by the details that occurred around the event—whether it be a season like winter or summer, a certain scent, specific sounds, or a visual picture forever stamped on our minds.

Darkness recognizes the way our mind works and how it is so intricately connected to our body, soul, and spirit. They realize that if they can assign a specific team—let's say, "The Time and Season Demons" to us, they can stir up our past with great effectiveness.

These hounds of darkness lurk in the shadows, patiently waiting till the calendar flips to their favourite time—your weak spot—the month or day or season a great hurt or sorrow struck your entire being and left you spiritually and emotionally crippled. They stealthily brush past you ever so slightly and stir little remnants of memory up through the smallest of details. It might be the sound of the train or the smell of the ground after a heavy rain. It may be a quick glimpse of a face that resembled someone from your past. There can be so many things which by themselves and in a different time are really insignificant. And isn't that how darkness works—using the apparently harmless and insignificant to usher in a devastating blow!

They seldom, or should I say 'never', knock on your front door and introduce themselves as 'demons of time and season' as they point to the calendar to remind you what you did or what tragedy happened at this time so many years ago. They are slicker than that. They wait and watch as they slip little chards of metal into your path but by the time you realize it, you have them all embedded in your feet. You fall to your knees, unable to carry on, bleeding and crippled as the flood of past memories, regrets, sorrows, and sadness threaten to wash you once again into a dark pit of hopelessness, despair, and isolation.

It is a wary believer that can overcome these demons. First, you must acknowledge the healing power of the Most High that covered your transgression or brought peace to you in your sorrow or loss.

Secondly, you must be aware of the times. Subconsciously mark on a calendar in your mind those times in the past that brought you low and note the events, faces, or stimuli from your senses that were associated with this time.

Thirdly, be sober—be alert—be on guard. Watch for your adversary. Watch and listen and be keen to pick up the subtle nuances of 'remembrances' with which he tries to stir up your mind or your emotions. When you identify them, rebuke the forces of darkness, bind them in Jesus' name and with the power of His blood, and deny them entry into your being through these stimuli.

We cannot afford to idly allow days to pass by and not be on the alert for this destroyer. He cannot take the Spirit of God from you, but he can disable a warrior by making him doubt the healing, restoration, forgiveness, and peace of his heavenly Father. It's as though darkness binds you to the past as if to a huge rock that is then flung into a deep pit. Slowly, the weight of the boulder drags you closer to the slippery edge where darkness hopes you lose all strength and footing and you plunge into the black hole of sadness, despair, and misery.

We must be aware of the schemes and tactics of Satan and his dark ones. The past cannot hold you unless you allow it to. We are to forget the past and press on to what lies ahead, conquering this place for the kingdom of God. A good warrior bandages his wounds and guards the tender spot from subsequent injury from the enemy as he continues to go forward—strong and secure—as he fights for his King.

Discernment

Those who know about the kingdom of God and have in their spirit a desire to walk more fully in the kingdom often desire the ability to discern the voice of God.

It appears that for most people, we readily hear and accept the voice of darkness—the voice that whispers criticism, condemnation, jealousy, anger, and shame. Many are quick to gather these subtly disguised tones of darkness and embrace them into their body and soul and spirit. They seem to have worn a path—like a well-used trail winding through a forest—into our innermost being where they then drop their subtle cloaks of seeming insignificance. Once there, they wield a powerful weapon specially forged for that particular soul in order to wound, immobilize, or destroy completely any embers of life that may have begun to grow.

These beginning whispers come very softly and inconspicuously at first; but left undetected, they gather strength as they travel through the worn paths in your body, soul, and spirit. These dark whispers from the enemy gather remnants left alongside the path—memories here and there from the past that summon up guilt, shame, and regret, or fears and concerns lying dormant alongside the trail. These stealthy dark ones have the accumulated wisdom they've gathered through the ages, and they access all their resources to gather from your thoughts, will, and emotions any little remnants lying quiet to use as reinforcements for their final task of dismantling or disabling your innermost being from ever attempting to walk fully in the kingdom of God and appropriating all the power of Jesus Christ that is available to you.

To a believer, the greatest gift of discernment is the ability to intercept such an attack on your own self before it gathers momentum and strength and puts in motion everything necessary to disable you from accessing the power of Christ which is working in you.

You see, darkness can't disable that power—that presence of Jesus Christ in you—on its own. All it can do is give you the gun and then set you up to shoot yourself. They have no real power over you. But you, on the other hand, have within yourself the ability to 'self-sabotage' the work begun—to turn off the flow of life from the Most High—simply by allowing the whispers of darkness to travel and wind through your body, soul, and mind gathering ammunition along the way and then detonating it in your spirit.

Discernment—identifying the enemy before he sets one step on the path to your spirit—is key. Second, after identification, comes annihilation. Destroy the whisperer before he gathers too much from your being. Cut him down with 'truth'—the truth of who you are in Christ—the righteousness of God; who you are—forgiven, free, and cleansed by the blood of Jesus Christ; who you are—called of God to manifest His glory and power in this place; who you are—a mighty soldier—vigilant, strong, and sure of your place in the army of the Most High, standing firm and tall beside the Son of God.

Many wish to hear the voice of God. Many desire the gift of discernment. Perhaps if we would stop listening to the voice of darkness that is set out to destroy us, we would more readily discern the voice of our Captain.

There is nothing noble about accepting thoughts of self-hate, shame, defeat, discouragement, or self-pity and allowing them to ruminate in our spirit like rotting, undigested food. These are from darkness.

Tune your ears to the voice of the Saviour. He speaks only truth, love, hope, and joy—any other thoughts you hear are from the whisperer of darkness.

STRENGTH FOR THE JOURNEY

Abandoned

ॐ

If Scripture is true and Jesus Himself said that He will never leave us nor forsake us, then why do so many believers feel at times abandoned and alone, or feel their heart cries are unheard by their heavenly Father?

Perhaps the answer lies in the fact that humans equate the actuality or reality of something in terms of feelings. People estimate and gauge success or failure or even the presence of God by feelings.

It is true that feelings are a gift from the Father—a seed—so to speak, that flowers into an outward expression. Feelings of love for your spouse flower into a passionate kiss or perhaps a warm embrace. Feelings of joy flower into a physical exuberance or energy and a sunny outlook on everything and everyone, showing itself through cheerfulness and encouragement. Feelings of peace and hope flower into a self-control and unshakeability even through challenging circumstances.

On the flip side, feelings not governed by Christ can show themselves as indifference and apathy, hopelessness, bitterness, and unexplainable anger. Feelings of anger may show their power through undeserved outbursts of nasty words and harshness directed at no one person in particular. Feelings of bitterness may present as cruel sarcasm and criticism and often later may manifest as a physical illness.

It is true that there are many contributing factors why we feel a certain way. Influences may originate from mental, emotional, or physical conditions or circumstances. However, we assume that God would always desire to make Himself known to us in a way that we could recognize easily through these times. After all, God is love and love is one of the strongest feelings known to man.

Sometimes we question that if God is so interested in us and so loving, why at times do we not 'feel' His presence and why does it happen when we need to hear or feel Him the most.

I believe the Scripture is true and God does not abandon us. However, I also believe He is a perfect loving Father who at times doesn't *reveal* His presence to us in order that we learn to walk by *faith* and not by *feeling,* to learn to 'fall into trust' in all the things we *know* about the Father, to strengthen our spiritual muscles and eyes and ears, to be able to walk with Jesus when we hurt, to be able to see His face and our path when all is dark around us, and to be able to hear His voice even through the heavy silence — because He is *still* there.

It's during times like these that you might ask yourself, "If I could feel, see, or hear my Saviour, what would He say to me?"

Sometimes it's like a child learning to ride a bike. When first starting out, he receives lots of support, encouragement, and steadying from his dad. Then gradually he is left on his own a little longer each time, able to bike on with a little more stability and confidence. But his dad is always there ready to set him back up should he take a tumble; ready to encourage him to steady his grip.

One day the child is ready to cross the streets and go to the store by himself. Although the child doesn't see him, his father is running alongside him, all the while keeping out of sight — maybe ducking behind a bush or tree. He listens to his child talk to himself as he comes to the intersection, "O.K. I can do this. Dad said to be sure to look both ways. O.K. I did that and no cars are coming so it's safe to cross." And off he goes safely across the road.

Did he feel his father's encouraging hand on his shoulder? Did he hear his father's instruction? Did he see his father's consenting glance? No. But he *remembered*—he remembered the times of love and care and instruction he felt when he was learning, and now he was confident that if his dad were actually with him at the crosswalk, he would hear him say, "You're doing fine, my child. You've remembered everything I've taught you. Good work. Keep on going."

Our heavenly Father is like that. He is constantly walking right beside you as you journey through the challenges that life brings. He is sitting right there beside you now as you wait in silence for direction. If He is your Saviour, He is living right inside you and whether you feel Him or not, when you remember His words to you, follow His ways for you, and recall His great love for you, you will be able to pass through this slice of time in your life where you may feel abandoned. You **will** pass through this time by keeping on the path 'by faith' and not 'by feeling'.

And if He would choose to reveal Himself to you in a very real way (and He may), He would say, "You're doing fine, My child. You are remembering all you've been taught. You are on the right track. Keep on going. I love you so much." He is watching you as you safely cross through this lonely time and come to the other side, stronger then ever before.

Through my walk with the Jesus, I can assure you that He will never leave you. But more importantly, Jesus Himself promises that "…I will not in any way fail you nor give you up nor leave you without support. [I will] not, [I will] not, [I will] not in any degree leave you helpless, nor forsake nor let [you] down, [relax My hold on you].—Assuredly not!" Hebrews 13:5 (AMP)

God Is Love

It is with hesitancy that I pick up my pen to even begin to write on such a subject as God's love for it is deeper and wider, higher and longer, and richer far than any word or thought expressed by human form.

Some use the phrase, "God is love," so casually that the true meaning has become dulled and obscure to our minds and souls.

Some use those three amazing words, "God is love," to silence their souls and spirits that gnaw at them within as they continue on their path of satisfying the sinful desires of their flesh and mind. They are quick to utter a conscious rebuke to their inner self by saying, "If God is love how could He allow me, as well as a lot of other people in this world, to go to hell just because we don't 'believe' in Him or aren't 'saved'?" To some—actually to many lost—this simple phrase, "God is love," has become a license to use His love as a safety net to catch them after they have walked the tightrope of sin and self and found themselves falling out of control to a certain death. No commitment, no surrender of self, no purity, no conscience of right and wrong on their part. "Just let me do as I please and I'm sure if You, God, are love, You'll forgive me—but I'll wait until I'm good and ready, and have done all I want to do."

How sad that three simple words carrying such profound power and healing and peace have been marketed to the world by darkness in such a way that God's love has been twisted into a carefree, care-less, 'do as you please because I love you,' 'flower-child' acceptance of sin, and an ignorance toward the price His love exacted and our responsibility to such an awareness.

Yes, God's love is always there—always ready to forgive, receive, and restore those who with the slightest desperate cry call out to Him. He is love. It is His nature. However, it involves an acknowledgement and repentance of our true condition in light of His holiness, and a receiving of His love and forgiveness.

The love of God can be illustrated by the sun that shines above us. It faithfully shines day in and day out—24 hours a day. However, sometimes it is dark overhead because the earth has rotated away from the sun. Sometimes the full warmth and light of the sun is not experienced because clouds or smog obstruct its radiant beams.

God's own love is like that. His love is continual, unending, always pouring down on us—24 hours a day, 7 days a week, day after day, week after week, and year after year.

One reason we do not experience the full radiant energy of His love is that there is an obstruction—some interference—between Him and us. Like the sun with clouds or smog obstructing its rays, God's rays of love can be obstructed by our own self. Perhaps it's feelings of unworthiness and self-hate that block His love from melting through. Perhaps our minds and hearts are full of smog—unholy thoughts and contemplations or unholy feelings of anger, bitterness, and jealousy—that form a barrier to His love. All these create a haze over our bodies, souls, and spirits, and the full heat and energy of the love of God cannot penetrate. We don't allow it to.

Perhaps we ourselves have 'rotated' like the earth and have literally turned our backs on God. We may have decided to live our own way first and when we have given everything a try, we'll maybe see if what God offers is any better. Perhaps He didn't 'measure up' to our expectations and demands. He didn't come through for us with what we asked from Him. Basically, we didn't get what we wanted, and so like a spoiled child, we cross our arms over our chest, stomp our feet, pull our lips into a pout, and turn our back on Him.

Does His love still pour down? Yes. Why? Because that is who He is. He is love and He cannot stop being who He is—no more then the sun can stop shining. It's just that the person who turns his back on the Father has turned away from receiving His love.

So how do we place ourselves back in the 'high noon' position of the radiant beams of the love of God? Well, on our own initiative and in our own strength that is rather difficult. And that is why the Father has sent a Helper—the Holy Spirit—to come alongside us and help us reposition ourselves and clear away the interferences so we are able to receive the love of God into our entire being to warm the cold, dark, secret places, to soften and melt the hurt and hardened heart, and to wash our body, soul, and spirit over with the warmth of His forgiveness and peace which surpasses—defies and goes beyond—all our human understanding.

What must we do to acquire this help from the Holy Spirit? What action must we take in order to place ourselves under the direct outpouring of God's love? The only action required is 'inaction'—quit striving, quit 'thinking,' and just surrender. Allow the gentle breeze of the breath of the Holy Spirit to blow the clouds and smog away. Just rest. Close your eyes and remember a time when you were laying on the warm sand of the beach. Your eyes were closed and the clouds were covering the full brightness of the sun. The sand had been warmed by the heat of the sun and you were able to relax and rest easily.

Then, gradually, although your eyes are closed, a brightness gradually begins to wash over you. Even with eyes closed, the brightness of the uncovered sun causes you to raise your hands to shelter your eyes from the strength of the rays of light. The intense heat warms your entire body and penetrates every pore — every inch of your being — and you can feel its warmth reaching deep inside. You are wrapped up so securely in the warmth and brightness that you don't want to move. You don't want to miss one second of this unexplainable warmth bearing down so gently on your being. It's as if the sun is shining just on you — and for you only.

This is what the Holy Spirit does. If you are willing to lay quiet and rest and allow Him to push aside all your cares and thoughts, worries and burdens, and to lift off the sin that has weighed you down, the pure love of the Father will soon pour over you and penetrate into the deepest parts of your soul and spirit.

To just receive — to take in — there is nothing you need to do, nothing you need to think, and nothing you need to conjure up within your spirit. Just stop — stop all striving — and receive. Let your spirit drink in the pure love of the Father. Let your soul find peace and rest in the pure love of God. Let your body rest and restore under the pure love of the Most High.

Remain and rest here in this place until you are so full you are overflowing, and when it is time to rise up and carry on with the tasks of life, you'll find that the radiance from the resting and receiving of the love of God has melted away the many weights that were bearing down on your whole being. You will walk through the day with the love of the Most High radiating from your face, through your words, and out through your actions.

There are no human words to express accurately and fully what it is like to receive the love of God. It is greater than our minds can comprehend but it is available for all who seek Him. Ask Him to help you receive the fullness of His presence, His love—Him alone.

Thank you, Father, that Your love is never failing—never ceasing—unstoppable. Thank you, Father, that regardless of where we are in our walk, what we have done or haven't done, You are constantly abiding, constantly pouring down You— pouring down Love—to refill, restore, and renew us from the inside out. Help us to rest before You and surrender to the Holy Spirit our whole being so He can scatter any interference or obstruction that may filter or screen Your love. Help us to receive Your love whereby we can then absorb You—Love—into ourselves—into our body, soul, and spirit.

A Faithful Friend

There is a verse in Scripture that tells us, "Faithful (blessed) are the wounds of a friend but deceitful (deadly) are the kisses of an enemy." (Proverbs 27:6) We have been taught through the years that this means that to desire and receive acceptance from an enemy will only result in harm to ourselves, but to receive admonition or constructive criticism from a friend—one who has our highest good in mind—will be a blessing to us, make us more complete in our being, or help us to become more Christ-like.

I believe that at times the Father allows wounds to be dealt from a 'friend' in order to accomplish a deep work within our spirits. I believe that nothing can compare to the indescribable pain and sorrow that comes from the hand of a friend who, unaware of their actions or words, wields a sword—a double-edged sword—that slices through your body, soul, and spirit with such force that it literally leaves you severed from yourself—a feeling of aching abandonment and aloneness — a ripping apart of the very things you felt were embedded and joined within both your beings. I'm not talking of material things — things that rust and decay over time. I'm speaking of spiritual and emotional things that flourish when you give your whole being to someone — a deep, deep level not fitly described with human language.

These are what I think sometimes are called the wounds of a friend. An oxymoron at its best for who would ever expect to be dealt such deadly blows from one whom you consider a friend — one who loves you no matter how you feel, or what you look like, or what you can or cannot do — truly unconditional love.

You know, a good friend is hard to find. One who remains by your side in season and out of season, through good and bad, through abundance and lack, through blessing and emptiness of soul. The Word of God describes such a One — a Friend who sticks closer than a brother, who promises never to leave or forsake us. But how do we rationalize the reality that such a Friend would ever permit such a wound, and how would it ever become a blessing?

For a faithful follower of Jesus, the wounding of the spirit is so very painful; yet I know the gentle hand of the Father can close the wound and miraculously heal it, and at times distance the memory of the wound in such a way as you find it difficult to summon up again the pain that seemed so fresh just a short time ago.

The faithfulness of a friend—Jesus—who would permit such a wound is seen through the healing, yes, but also as He works through the rest of your being. You see, because we are flesh and our nature is sinful, our flesh loves to hang on to the pain—the insult, the rejection, the abuse, the hurt—that has been dealt to us. Our flesh loves to rehearse the events over and over again, loves to conjure up all the past experiences that have brought pain to us, until we gather a grand collection of hurts and injuries to review while our spirit man begins to crumble and question the justice and sovereignty of a loving God.

You see, the flesh is at enmity with the spirit. The flesh, if allowed to control us and have dominion, is set to throw our spirit off the scent of God, His sovereignty, and His plan for our development as children of God. So now that the spirit of man is being sovereignly healed and restored, the flesh is ranting and raving and grasping at all the past and present injustices, hurts, tears, and sorrows, desperately trying to pry our own spirit from the healing peace and power that the Father is providing.

So I say to you who are in deep sorrow from a wound: Your spirit can and will be healed through the power of the Spirit of God. The pain you are most likely feeling is the pain that accompanies surgery—specifically amputation of the flesh—that sinful part of us that thrives in self-pity, pain, hurt, and remembrances of past injuries — that dark side of us that secretly desires to sabotage the work of the Father that brings about death to ourselves (our flesh) and brings us into a surrendered, flourishing, abandoned life in Christ Jesus.

As Paul said, "For you have died (*your flesh is falling away*) and your life (*your inner man*) is hidden with Christ in God (*under the protection and security of a most faithful Friend*)." (Colossians 3:3) (Italics are my words) He is faithful due to the fact that He who began this work in your spirit has promised He will perfect it until the day of Christ Jesus. He will perfect it even through the pain He permits as He wields the sword to sever parts of your flesh from its deadly hold on your life in order to strengthen your spirit.

Our Friend, Jesus, will show His love and faithfulness to us through pain and wounds, and we will feel His healing and strengthening in the weak and torn places. Although difficult, we are now able to understand the vital importance of His desire to sever the flesh from our being so He can have more of us and we can have less of ourselves — so that the "surpassing greatness of the power may be of God and not from ourselves." (II Corinthians 4:7b)

The Anonymous One

I am sure many of you have heard the prophetic words regarding the rising of a faceless and nameless generation that will take their place in the battle lines and raise their weapons against dark spiritual forces as if they had been fighting for years along with the rest of the more infamous warriors of our time. The power of the Holy Spirit will descend upon them with such force and energy that many will be taken back by the miraculous signs and wonders that are manifested through them.

For those who are 'nameless and faceless,' it seems not to matter that they are so because their focus—their passion—lies in the power of God working through them to accomplish whatever He desires. They have no desire in themselves for compensation or recognition; no desire to make a name or a place for themselves in this world's estimation of greatness or notoriety.

Why are they referred to as nameless and face-less? I believe it is because they have been kept in a secret place of the Most High being taught in the school of the Holy Spirit through the many lessons brought to them amid their individual and different life experiences. They haven't been out pushing their way into the public eye with their 'ministry' or their 'anointing,' hoping and striving for recognition and significance among the current list of movers and shakers in the religious world. They don't desire the cosmopolitan face and wardrobe or the glossy promotional paraphernalia that often accompanies up and coming celebrities, making sure they are just one notch above the latest craze or idol. They have been in boot camp and have come to the realization that all that really matters is Jesus Christ and Him alone. Not them, or their struggles, or their successes, or their ministries—nothing—nothing but the glory of Jesus Christ pouring into them and out through their very lives. They are being led through the course alone with only the Holy Spirit to guide, encourage, and strengthen them for the time ahead when they will be called out to take back from darkness that which belongs to the children of Light.

It is interesting, however, that those warriors are referred to as faceless and nameless simply because they are unknown. No one is aware of the trials and lessons they have been through that have been used to train their hands and minds for battle. If seen from the Lord's perspective, they would not be called 'name-less or faceless'. Instead they would be referred to as 'stealth warriors' — warriors who although they may lay dormant for a time, without much fanfare and notice, rise up and take the enemy off guard as they unleash all the power of the Holy Spirit that has been poured into them during their time in obscurity.

Am I part of that faceless, nameless generation? Are you one of those who to the world bare no significant or renowned name and no familiar or well-known face?

How do you know if you are one of the 'anonymous ones' appointed to live in seclusion until your King calls you out to battle?

There are certain tell-tale signs of those whose hearts beat in unison with the Spirit. You may wonder why you feel such an overwhelming yearning for more of the Saviour. You cannot seem to quench your hunger for Him and His Word. The Word of God becomes your sustenance — your very life — and when you read and meditate on it, His Word not only speaks to your soul but attaches or clings to your very spirit and becomes part of you. It seeps out of your heart through your words, and everyday life occurrences take on a new dimension as you seem to almost naturally begin to filter them through the Word.

You may find your spirit aches when you see the effects of sin reeking havoc upon the lives of others through disease, depression, broken relationships, pain, and sorrow.

You may wonder why your spirit rises up in you when you hear religious men and women preach about Jesus Christ and how following Him will bring prosperity and success to your life and business and make your life a veritable rose garden, but fail to preach the full counsel of God—the healing, redemptive, victorious power of Jesus Christ over sin and the power of Satan in one's life that allows them to live unbound to their own fleshly passion, pride, and sin?

You ask yourself, "Where are the preachers of righteousness and holiness? Why do so many preachers only represent Jesus Christ as a Saviour who casually brushes sin and godlessness under the carpet and pulls out a bag of religious treats and 'feel good' gifts to coddle the sin-soaked spirit and soul instead of preaching repentance and cleansing that comes only through the precious blood of Jesus?"

Why do these things throb endlessly in your spirit? Why is there no single thing in this world that will hush the torrent of thoughts and passion that gush up from your spirit and bring into question views and teachings that have been accepted by the religious masses for years? Why is there nothing that satisfies your soul like hiding away in quietness with the Word of God and the Holy Spirit to guide revelation and bring into understanding the downward slop on which this world seems to be sliding?

Understanding these thoughts and questions may lie in the awareness that you may indeed be a 'stealth warrior'. You have been stamped, sealed, and delivered into the Lord's army. Before you were even born, God knew you and destined you to be unsatisfied until He had pre-eminence and predominance in your spirit—your life. He placed inside your spirit a burning ember of passion for Jesus Christ. He stamped you with His seal and until you align yourself with the will of the Father for your life (actually His life through you), you will feel unsatisfied and discontent with all that surrounds you. Your life may give the appearance of being full and vibrant to those around you, but until you surrender your spirit to the call of the Spirit of God on your life, you find it dull and meaningless. The Father created you for something unique—perhaps not something famous by this world's standards—but something unique for Him to work through to reveal His glory and power.

He looked into your spirit before you were born and that simple gaze penetrated and left a mark—an imprint—on your life. Before you came to this earth, He knew everything about you. He knew you and loved you when you were barely the size of a marble cradled in the warmth of your mother's womb. He knew you and loved you when you were a tiny baby totally dependent on someone else for food, love, and protection. He knew you and loved you when you nervously set out on that first day of school. He knew you and loved you when you would ride your bike around town with your friends and search for frogs and snakes and butterflies. He knew you and loved you when you would daydream about the boy or girl next to you in class. He knew you and loved you when you made choices that took you away from His ways of holiness and purity. He knew you and loved you when you, for a season, left the things that you knew were right and true and followed the common path which so many others take. He knew you and loved you when you were angry with Him because you felt He let you down or abandoned you and your dreams. He knew you and loved you when you surrendered your life anew to Him and sought His forgiveness and restoration. He knows what the next day or year or decade holds for you and what you will do with it—and He loves you. He fully knows you now—today—and His love for you is continuing to pour down on you at this very moment.

And on Calvary over 2000 years ago, Jesus Christ, the Holy Son of the Most High God, bore the sin that kept you bound. Not only yours, but that of the whole world. There on that cross, I believe He held your face in his hands once again and the pure energy of His love poured out on you as He paid the price of sin and death and when you accepted His gift, He set you free from its hold on your life. You became a new creation and the grip of sin and death was broken. You became an heir—a son or daughter—of the Most High God. The Word of God says that He has you inscribed on the palms of His hands. (Isaiah 49:16)

In that moment when you received His gift of salvation and the Holy Spirit took up residence in your spirit, that small ember burst into a flame that has been growing ever since. It has been continually fed from the Word of God and the work of the Holy Spirit within you. At times, the passion and power of the Holy Spirit burns so intensely that you scarcely can hold it in. People do not suspect that underneath that common exterior and behind that 'normal' life, there beats a heart of a warrior—someone who is willing to sacrifice all they have and all they are for the sake and glory of Jesus Christ. And the day will come when you will be summoned by the Most High and will rise up from among them and with power and strength from on high, do battle for your King. And when the battle is over, you will slip away into obscurity until called upon once again.

Stealth warriors—many are surprised at who they are and where they have come from. Isn't that God's way at times—choosing the 'unsuspecting' to accomplish His work? For you, it doesn't matter who knows your name or recognizes your face. All that matters is that people see Jesus Christ in you, they recognize His reflection—His glory—on you, and they are impacted by His power flowing through you.

It is true that for many, they see only the outward appearance of a man although the Lord truly looks on the heart, for even in the Christian realm, names and faces seem to count for something, seem to lend significance, authority, power, and credibility to the message or ministry. How unfortunate that many worthy soldiers, many valiant and faithful warriors of Jesus Christ are passed over by those who see only the outer visage and take no time to look—to really look—into their soul and spirit. If they did, they wouldn't see just another person trying to serve the best they could in their own strength. They would see Jesus there. They would see His face on their face. They would see His compassion and love and strength in their eyes. They would see His name written over their hearts and sense the power of the Holy Spirit coursing through them. They would recognize that this one carries not his own identity but has taken on the identity of Jesus Christ as his own.

Nameless and faceless—not you—not at all—for on you is written the name of Jesus Christ and through your life is manifested His glory. You will join the ranks of the faithful 'anonymous ones' like Antipas, although unmentioned in any other historical writings except Revelation 2:13, is lovingly and intimately known to the Most High as "My witness, My faithful one."

And on that day when we come before our King and His glory shines around us brighter than the noonday sun, we will bow down before Him and in honour and reverence lay our crowns at His feet. Then there will be only one name that matters—the Name at which every knee shall bow and tongue confess—that beautiful name of JESUS.

Mr. Tippit

I wonder if anyone remembers the game from some years ago that was played in many households by many children and adults alike. It featured a character known as Mr. Tippit who would be balanced upside down on his nose with legs apart. The object of the game was on each player's turn to place a disc on one of the extended legs and hope that Mr. Tippit wouldn't tip it! Great care was taken with each turn as it was a delicate case of balance and precision that would keep poor Mr. Tippit balancing so precariously on his little nose.

You know, life isn't so much different from that little game. In fact, I think that game was probably based on someone's profound insight into humanity who, with tongue in cheek, devised a game to poke some fun at our feeble attempt to maintain all the challenges life brings to us without losing our 'balance'—our sense of 'stability' through it all.

I believe life has become a balancing act—with emphasis on the word 'act'—for most of us. You see, I believe that since the fall of mankind through the one act of disobedience committed in the Garden of Eden, we have been struggling to keep in balance our lives from toppling over and us having to admit something is not quite right with us and in us.

At creation mankind was designed to live in total stability and balance. I believe that the Most High created man with three distinct but interdependent facets of his being—the body, the soul (mind, will, and emotions), and the spirit. This is much like a triangle with the large base representing the spirit of mankind—a large base that gives balance and strength and stability to the rest of our being. The middle segment of the triangle would represent the soul—the seat of our mind or thought processes and reasoning, the emotions, and the will. The tip of the triangle would then be seen as the body—the flesh—which is simply a vehicle to carry our soul and spirit and to enjoy the wonderful creation given to us by the Father. It was His good intention that we live primarily in the strength of our spirit—our spirit which in the beginning was in peaceful communion with our Creator—and that our body and soul live as extensions of our healthy spirit.

Unfortunately, through sin and time, the triangle has become inverted. Darkness has crept in and tipped the strength of our being upside down so that most of us are now living life as a balancing act, trying so very carefully not to upset our body or our soul as we deal with the weights that life places on us. If only we could somehow 'flip' the triangle back over onto its strong, secure base and put into perspective and balance the rest of our being.

Can it ever be done?

I believe it can. But it won't come through our own strength or our own maneuvering through all the self-help regimes out there in the world. All our focus on 'balancing' and 'managing stress in an overstressed world' will not accomplish any significant long term change. Sure, a retreat away to a quiet cottage or even a welcome change of scenery will do a body good but it is only a 'band aid' approach to a sick spirit.

Our spirits are sick. They are dying of suffocation and inactivity. They have become weak and lazy and in that state will accept any little tidbit of relief thrown their way to relieve the agony of inactivity. Our spirits have become incapacitated, cut off from performing the task for which they were created. We all know the frustration that comes when we realize what we want to 'do' with our lives but are unable to see it come to pass. Magnify that feeling over years and years and you will begin to realize how weak and discouraged and sick our spirits have become.

In the meantime, our body and soul have taken the lead. Usually it is the body first. "Fill me up—feed me, make me feel good, meet my need!" it screams at us daily. "Clean me, make me smell nice. Do I look o.k.? Do I look better than so-and-so?" Our soul clamors for a prime position too. "Does anyone know how intelligent I really am? Does anyone see that I know the answer to all their problems? Will someone please make my heart leap with joy and excitement? Will someone please fill up my 'emotional tank'? I am so lonely and empty but I will continue to give the appearance of being 'together' because my very life—my very existence—depends on their response to me. I don't care what is right any more. All I know is that I must get ahead. I must succeed. I WILL succeed in this life no matter what or who gets in my way. I WILL get what I want out of life—a beautiful body, a beautiful home, a fast car, a successful business, a fabulous yearly holiday to Hawaii, a huge bank account so I can show and tell to everyone that I AM hanging on. I am doing well. I am balancing this life excellently. I have not become another failed 'Mr. Tippit' who finds himself unable to hold up the charade of a life that's seemingly 'all together'. I will not be found laying helpless and alone among the rubble of what used to be my trophies in life that suddenly came crashing down around me like building blocks once built so tall and straight but then toppled under the strain of supporting that final block resting so precariously on top."

What has happened to us? What has set us off course so drastically? How did we ever get to this sad and desperate point in our human existence? Was it sudden? Is it just the pressures of this technological age? Are we weaker than our ancestors who died for their families and forged through sickness and tragedy and yet came through all these things with faith in God intact and a love for life and family?

Can we ever possibly tip the triangle over and get 'life' in balance once more?

Again, I say it is possible. Not with our own well-concocted schemes and formulas and self—help programs. Not in reliance on our own high-minded-ness. It is possible only through the blood of Jesus Christ and the power of the Holy Spirit.

Until we come to the point where we realize that nothing we do is working, life will remain futile and empty. Jesus Christ alone can fill that void, that emptiness, that ache in our spirits that cries for someone, anyone, to pull us out of this dark pit in which we are trapped. If you have not yet realized the saving power of Jesus Christ, it is vitally important for you to understand this today. If you are honest with yourself, you know that all the things you have tried in this life have left you still longing for something more. Jesus Christ is your answer. He is waiting for you to admit your helplessness—your inability to fill the hole in your heart. He gave His life on Calvary for you. He paid the price we could not pay in order that, through accepting His gift of salvation, He would give us life and life more abundantly. Acknowledge your sin, acknowledge your need of Him, and accept His gift of Life. Accept His forgiveness and His healing.

The greatest healing, apart from salvation of a lost soul, is the reversal of our being. It is surrendering the complete man — body, soul, and spirit — to the Holy Spirit so He can 'rearrange' us. It's like wiping out a hard drive because of a virus and then restarting the computer back up. If you've ever done this, you will know that it takes a bit of work but when it is up and running again, it is quicker and you know the system is 'clean'.

What can we do?

I believe we can start by identifying how darkness has 'flipped' us. Identification of a sickness is the first step to recovery. Perhaps it's time to get personal. Who runs your being? Is it your flesh? Is it your thoughts, emotions, or what you want (will)? Is it your spirit? Is your spirit co-joined with the Spirit of God? Identify what makes you feel and act and think the way you do? What is your motivation in your life? Which part of your being do you listen to?

I must stress at this point that unless you are filled with the Spirit of God, there is little benefit for you to consider 'flipping' the triangle of your being. Without the pure, Holy Spirit of God controlling our spirit, we are opening our inner selves up to the spiritual realm of darkness. Darkness mimics the Light. Great care and consideration must be given to this area. If you are not filled with the Holy Spirit I urge you now to seek the Lord on this vital point. A life not controlled by the Spirit of Life will be open to receive instruction and guidance from the spirit of darkness.

If you have surrendered your entire being to the Spirit of God and have been baptized in the Spirit, then pray for protection and guidance to lead you through the process of re-establishing the 'balance' in your life.

The Creator has indeed given us a marvelous gift in the form of our body, soul, and spirit. His intentions were that we enjoy fellowship with Him, enjoy His creation, and to represent His glory in every aspect of our existence. He has given us the tools to operate this marvelous machine of ours so that it can run smoothly and perform that for which it was created.

Start with a little step.

When in prayer, speak to your body and remind it of its amazing construction. Thank the Lord for your body and then speak to it, telling it is no longer 'running the show' but it must return to its proper position in your being. It is an extension of your healthy soul and spirit.

Next, speak to your soul—your mind, will, and emotions—and thank the Lord for the way in which

He has made you able to reason, to express feelings, to desire good things. Remind your soul of its proper placement in your being; that your spirit is now taking its rightful place working along with the Spirit of God; and that your soul will be able to function much better now that the Spirit of God is allowed to filter through Himself and the Word of God all that comes into your mind, will, and emotions.

Lastly, commune with your spirit and the Spirit of God. Release your spirit to soar with the Spirit of God and to be free. Allow healing, peace, and restoration to flood your spirit. Allow the Holy Spirit to minister to you, to love you, to guide, direct, and protect you.

You see, our bodies and souls are reflections of our spirits. When we exhibit sickness, disease, stress, anxiety, anger, or other 'ills' in our body and soul, it is simply a sign that our spirits are sick.

Our spirits need a touch from the Holy Spirit— Holy—meaning pure, undefiled, and perfect. A Holy Physician able to heal with the most loving touch. Learn to work with the Holy Spirit to 're-order' your self—to put back into rightful place all the aspects of your being—and then allow the Holy Spirit to direct your life through your spirit.

No one can win at Mr. Tippit forever. Sooner or later, he will fall over and all the chips will scatter across the floor.

Life is not a game. It is a beautiful expression of the heart of the Most High. It is a representation of His glory and power and majesty. We, with the aid of the Most High, can be these earthen vessels that carry about the glory of the Lord. He will be seen through our body, our soul, and our spirit if we allow Him to set us back up on our solid base—on the Solid Rock—where there is stability, security, power, and peace to live out our days in this place as intended.

The Journey

A long time ago, there was a young man who left his father to go on a long journey into the land beyond his home. The young man loved his father and the father loved his son. Before setting out on his journey, the father gave the young man a letter penned from his own hand which told of his love for him, told of the dangers of the land beyond, and reminded him of the time they had spent together— talking, laughing, and sharing while sitting on the porch as the warmth of the streaming rays of sunshine surrounded them.

The young man stuffed the letter into his pocket and determined to read it later for now it was time to leave. Life was calling him to the land beyond, and he desired to travel far from the safety and security of his home to fill the longing in his heart for something more. He had heard of the adventures in the world afar, and although he loved his father and felt he would never lose the memory of moments together, part of him yearned for what everyone else was experiencing.

Many years had passed since the young man had left. The father continued to wait in the little cabin in the clearing. Daily he would sit on the porch and the warmth of the streaming rays of sunshine would surround him as he gazed off into the distance — waiting — longing for the familiar form of his son to crest the hill that seemed to separate their worlds.

The years of time had taken their passage on the young man's form. He had indeed experienced many adventures in the world beyond. In the beginning, he would reach into his pocket and read with longing the letter written from his father. It brought him some comfort and rest from the swirl of the world around him. There were battles, and the young man did experience the ravages of war upon his being. He walked with a limp now and his body bore the scars of many struggles. After the time of battle, there were other adventures in the path of the young traveler. He worked hard in the city to provide for himself, all the while trying as best he could to stay clear of those who tried to weigh him down with their sense of hopelessness and despair.

The young man began to gather things he needed to survive and with which to protect himself during his journeys. He knew now that traveling alone was safer than the company of those who meant him no good. He carried with him a pack into which he stuffed many needful items he secured along his way. These were valuable to him for he could not make it without them.

The young man had traveled many places. He had trodden the path through the desert, drinking sparingly from the canteen in his pack. He had weathered the beating rain and cold wind, and often covered himself from the raging storms with the old blanket also stuffed into his bulging pack. He forged through cold, swift running rivers that almost swept him over only to crawl up onto the bank and dry himself by a small fire started by a piece of flint he collected on his travels. Long, winding paths through mountain passes were made a little easier with the help of a walking stick he had carved from an old branch of a tree under which he rested one day. And then there were the weapons. He carefully guarded the small, sharp stones and jagged arrowheads hewn from flat pieces of rock for they provided him with food through hunting and fishing. He also needed to protect himself from beasts of all kinds, and to do this he needed an effective weapon — one that was strong, reliable, and lethal. Of all his belongings, this weapon was the one he depended upon the most for his safety and survival.

As time pressed on and continued to wear on the young man, he drew less and less upon the letter stuffed in the bottom of his pocket. One day, however, while searching for something to make a small fire by which to warm himself, he came once again upon the letter. He had forgotten — it had been so long since he had read it. He gingerly opened the tattered paper and tears streaked the dirty face of the young man — once strong and confident, but now tired, weak, lame, and empty.

He read again the letter penned tenderly by his father who wrote of his love for him, who warned him of the dangers and traps of the world beyond, and who reminded him of the time spent together on the porch as the warmth of streaming rays of sunshine would surround them as they talked and laughed and shared each other's company.

Then, in that moment, something happened to the young man. He resolutely wiped the tears from his face, carefully refolded the letter, and gently placed it in the safety of his pocket. There was a light — a small ember — beginning to glow deep within him. He had not felt this for such a long time. At first he was unsure and a little frightened by the warmth with which the ember gave. Then, slowly, he began to remember more and more the place by his father's side on the porch. The memories began to flood back into his mind and stir his soul. He would — he determined — he would return to his father. He desired his father — to feel again the warmth of his embrace, to sit again in the peacefulness of his presence on the sun bleached porch, to share and talk and laugh and be free from all the heaviness he had accumulated through his travels.

He hadn't realized how heavy his heart had become nor the weight of his pack he carried in and out of each day filled with all the things he needed to protect himself, to survive in the world beyond. He hadn't realized until now how much this world had wore him down and taken its toll on his body, mind, and spirit.

With a spring in his step and a faint glimpse of a smile on his tear-stained face, the young man gathered his pack, his stick, and his weapon and headed as best he could toward home. It was funny, he thought, that although he had traveled so long and so far from home that once he had determined to return, he seemed to instinctively know which path to take, which mountain pass to cross, across which river to forge, and which cities and byways to avoid. It was as if he was drawn to his home.

His journey home was not without obstacles. Distractions from every side seemed to come at him—old remembrances of places he had passed through—old temptations of adventures that had brought him some momentary relief in his tired and lonely moments. But with great determination in his heart, he shook off the old desire to try again the things that once seemed to satisfy his longing in his soul. With greater resolve, he picked up his pace knowing that soon he would be on the path that would lead to his father.

Familiar surroundings of home soon began to pass the young traveler by. He was close to home now. He could feel it. He could almost smell the smoke gently curling from the chimney. He could see in his mind—his father. Would he be waiting for him still? It had been so long since he had seen him. The young man had taken no effort to write to him over the long time since he had been gone. Did his father think he had been killed or lost? Would his father remember him? Would he remember the times together on the porch with the warmth of streaming rays of sunshine surrounding them as they talked and laughed and shared and loved each other?

Heavy clouds of doubt began to steal over his heart and mind, and an uneasy fear settled into his soul. Pausing on the path, knowing that over the next hill was the home of his father, the young man remained so very still—as if fear and doubt had immobilized him. Unable to take even one more step toward home, the young man looked back toward the trail behind him. He knew what it held. He knew the price the years had taken on him in every way.

He looked again at the faintly worn path leading to the top of the hill. Nothing could be worse then where he had come from—the loneliness, the hunger, the danger, the toil and struggle. If he forged on, he would at least know if he ever had the chance of finding rest in his father again. To live in regret of never knowing if his father was waiting for him over the hill would be as death to him. With slow, deliberate steps he continued upward, slowly cresting the top of the hill.

In the valley below the other side of the hill, gentle wisps of smoke curled from the chimney atop of a small cabin. Sitting on the porch was a figure — waiting. Waiting as he had for many, many years.

Looking out from the cabin in the valley, a waiting father caught sight of a small figure seeming to become larger as it crested the hill. Soon the limping, tired frame of the young man stood on the top of the hill. The father never moved his gaze from the young man's form. He rose from his chair and stood at the edge of the porch. He lifted his hands to cover the glare of the sun from his eyes.

The young man didn't move. His hands dropped to his side and he just stood there — so very still. A myriad of feelings rushed over him, and he was unable to discern one from another; but they seemed to sweep him up in one fell swoop such that he began to pick up his gait. He could hardly wait! His fast trot moved quickly into a desperate run. But he was hindered — he was burdened down with his pack and all the things he had collected over his journey. Without a thought, he dropped his walking stick and although limping, he continued to run quickly toward his father. Next, he threw his weapon down. He had not thought of its importance now — father was there. Shaking the pack from off his shoulders, it dropped with a thud to the ground. The young man didn't waste any time to check to see if his once precious items were safe. He twisted his arms out of his dirty, worn coat and threw it to the ground.

His father was watching and his eyes were filled with tears—not sad ones—but the deepest kind of love and joy tears anyone could shed. He held out his strong arms to his son. The young man almost stumbled as his feet couldn't keep up with his heart to reach his father's embrace. Collapsing into his father's arms, the son melted upon his shoulder and sobbed great sobs of relief. He had made it home and, yes, his father was still there—waiting, longing for him—just for him.

Wiping the tears from his son's face, the father led the young man up onto the porch. Finding their old familiar spot to sit, the father took the son's face in his hands and looked deep into his eyes. "You found your way home, my child. I have been waiting for you—longing for your return for so very long." The son rested his head on his father's lap as warm rays of streaming sunshine surrounded them.

The father and the son spent many minutes, hours, and days enjoying the company of one another. In time—and it seemed to the son as if not much time had passed—the limp in the young man began to disappear. Scars and wounds that once marked the body of the son were slowly dissolving and replaced with clean, clear, healthy skin. The desperate, tired, faraway look that came from deep within the soul of the son was soon replaced with the brightness of joy and peace and rest. His eyes sparkled at the sight of his father, and a warm smile adorned his face.

It wasn't long until the son was strong once again. And, yes, there were responsibilities of life that took the young man away from home. But it was different this time. He never left the cabin without spending time with his father—talking, laughing, sharing and just being in his company. Somehow, it gave the son the strength to go out and do what he had to do. He made sure he never traveled so far away that he couldn't return to the father's house to once again sit in the warm rays of streaming sunshine that enveloped them as they communed together.

I wonder, how far have we traveled from the Father? Have we been drawn so far away from Him that we barely remember the time we first sat at His knee and were soaked in His love? Have we accumulated a pack full of life's necessities to ensure we make our way through to the next stop? What kind of things do we carry in our packs? Some carry all the material things they have accumulated, thinking they will be able to secure their future with them. Some carry many people—collecting people and relationships—depending on their company to quell the discontent in their soul which cries for that one relationship that will never disappoint. Some carry years of bitterness and hurt that propel them onward to succeed, perhaps to cover the pain of rejection and aloneness. Some have scars of wounds and injuries that they have incurred at the hands of others. Some carry walking sticks on which to lean when their own strength runs dry.

What do you carry to replace the Father?

Perhaps, if you listen with your heart, you can hear him calling you to His side. Perhaps you're at the point in your life now that you realize all the things you thought would carry you through are actually a burden to you because you are in reality carrying them. You carry them to replace—to substitute—the life-giving relationship with the Father. Perhaps it's time to lighten the load—to let go of the things you have carried so long—to return to the knee of the Father and find the rest you so desperately need.

Picture yourself, now, at the top of the hill, looking down upon the cabin. There is the Father—the One you knew so intimately so long ago. The One who loves you more than all the love you found in all your journeys through the world. Deep in your soul you are drawn to Him —you desire once again that sweet communion. You know, too, that He is longing for you, and that He has never stopped waiting for you to return. Now it is time to choose. Choose to let go of the heavy pack, the stick, and weapons of defense that have been your security in the past. One by one you drop them to the ground as you make your way to the Father.

You see His arms outstretched and with relief from the weight of needless burdens removed, you run to His embrace. Your heart and soul leap within you, and the warmth of His love is likened to rays of warm sunshine that engulf your entire being. He holds your precious face in His strong, warm hands and He whispers your name. Yes, *your* name. Just the sound of your name coming from His lips soothes your tired and weary spirit and ushers in a flood of safety and rest into your soul. You are home now.

Listen to the voice of the Father bring healing to your soul and spirit. Receive His words that touch the depths of your being and bring life again.

Rest in Him.

Printed in the United States
93654LV00001B/358-603/A

9 781604 770780